Her scream pierced the night....

As the man raised his hand high, Amber saw the silver glimmer of the knife blade beneath the pale yellow glow of the moon.

The blade began to move; then suddenly the man with the deadly dark eyes was wrenched away from her.

It was Michael. He'd come to her rescue, as she had prayed.

He stood there now on the deck, hands on his hips, cold blue fire in his eyes. He towered above the others, arrogant, assertive, in control.

"Michael!" she whispered as she threw herself into his arms. "Thank God!"

He caught her, holding her stiffly, pushing her away. "No, Amber," he said softly. "I'm sorry. I'm not here to help you."

She had never felt so betrayed in all her life.

Dear Reader:

As usual, we've gathered the cream of the crop for you this month in Silhouette Intimate Moments. Start off with Beverly Sommers and the first book in a terrific new trilogy, "Friends for Life." In *Accused* she tells the story of Jack Quintana, a man accused of a murder he didn't commit. His defender is Anne Larkin, a woman whose memories of Jack are less than fond. As they work together to clear his name, however, they discover that love isn't necessarily the most logical of emotions. In the next two months, look for *Betrayed* and *Corrupted*, the stories of Anne's friends Bolivia and Sandy. These three really are *friends for life*.

Also this month, Heather Graham Pozzessere returns with *A Perilous Eden*, a story of terror on the high seas and passion under the hot Caribbean sun. It's an adventure not to be missed. Lee Magner brings you *Sutter's Wife*, the story of a make-believe marriage that quickly becomes the real thing. Finish the month with new author Dee Holmes and *Black Horse Island*, a stunning debut performance from a writer to watch.

In coming months, look for new books by Emilie Richards, Barbara Faith, Marilyn Pappano and Jennifer Greene, not to mention fall treats from, among others, Linda Howard, Kathleen Korbel and Patricia Gardner Evans. Something great is always happening at Silhouette Intimate Moments.

Leslie J. Wainger
Senior Editor

A Perilous Eden

HEATHER GRAHAM POZZESSERE

Silhouette Intimate Moments

Published by Silhouette Books New York

America's Publisher of Contemporary Romance

SILHOUETTE BOOKS
300 East 42nd St., New York, N.Y. 10017

ISBN: 0-373-07328-3

First Silhouette Books printing March 1990

Printed in the U.S.A.

HEATHER GRAHAM POZZESSERE

considers herself lucky to live in Florida, where she can indulge her love of water sports like swimming and boating year-round. Her background includes stints as a model, actress and a bartender. She was once actually tied to the railroad tracks to garner publicity for the dinner theater where she was acting. Now she's a full-time wife, mother of four and, of course, a writer of historical and contemporary romances.

Prologue

The Alexandria, *International Waters*
June 15, 12:45 a.m.

The night was black. The sky, the horizon, the earth—everything was black for as far as the eye could see. Standing by the ship's railing, feeling the sea breeze pick up her hair and toss it softly around her face, Amber was aware for long moments only of the enormity of the sea by night, of the total blackness that seemed like an aching void, mystical, frightening, and still . . . enchanting.

Then she began to hear the sounds.

Little sounds. Soft, muffled, furtive. They were so quiet that they took some time to penetrate the fog of her absorption, and when they did, it was their furtive and sinister nature that made her whirl around at last. And then she recognized the sounds, of course.

They had been made by a small boat coming to rest beside the ocean liner. By the stealthy climb of men up to the deck. By footsteps.

She hadn't been alone on deck. Senator Daldrin had come out much as she had, to stare out at the night.

But he was no longer alone.

"Stop!" Amber shouted. "Stop! Help!"

Shouting made no impression. She threw back her head and screamed again, loudly, desperately, with all the strength and will in her being. Her fingers dug into the ship's railing, and she prayed that her screams would be heard over the beating of the drums from the nearest lounge. The wind caught her scream, lifted it and carried it away. The only ones who seemed to hear her were the dark wraiths now moving so fleetly toward the black-jacketed form of Senator Daldrin.

"Stop!" Amber shouted again, her heart pounding like the muffled drumbeats. She tried to sound indignant and assertive. "Leave him alone! Who are you? What are you doing? Help! Leave that man alone, or you'll be arrested!"

The swift, furtive wraiths ignored her.

Where had they come from? she wondered with amazement. The *Alexandria* was out at sea—far from any port. The black-clad figures didn't seem real. They were creatures from the void of the night, imaginary, illusions. It was easy to imagine things here, for nothing in the world was like the darkness of a night at sea. Not even the cruise ship's elaborate lighting could dispel that darkness for more than a few feet.

The men were not imaginary. They were real, and there were four of them, large, anonymous in their black sweaters and jeans and ski caps. They didn't even glance her way, and yet, as she watched them in dismay and astonishment, she felt the icy finger of fear slide down her spine. These men were nothing so soft as illusion. There was a cold-blooded determination and purpose to their movements.

Senator Daldrin had turned. He was a handsome man, tall and silver-haired, dignified. He saw the four figures coming toward him, and his eyes widened, the only sign of alarm that he gave.

"Amber, get the hell out of here!" he roared to her.

Get out? She couldn't. She was the only chance of help the senator had. She had to stay. Had to do something.

"Stop, damn you, or I'll—" Amber began, her fingers laced tightly around the railing. Stop or else what? What was she going to do against four men who'd had the ability to board the ship straight out of the night?

She spun around then, looking toward the lights of the aft lounge. Michael, she thought. Michael Adams.

Michael, where the hell are you? she wondered feverishly.

Sometimes it seemed that she had seen no one but him since she had come aboard the *Alexandria*. Or perhaps it was just that his presence alone was so quietly dominating that she saw no one else when he was near. Or maybe it was because she had been slowly falling in love with him. No, not slowly at all, and maybe it wasn't love. Maybe it was just the shocking, shattering attraction that pulsed all around them whenever they met.

Curiously, she had first seen him in Washington. They had passed by one another on the path at the Smithsonian, and several minutes later she had found herself remembering the face of a passerby. It was a unique face, and he was a unique man, even if she couldn't completely comprehend what made him so. Not his features, for they were ordinary enough. His eyes were blue, a light, ice blue against his tanned skin. His hair was a tawny color. There was strength in his face; everything was put together pleasantly enough. He wasn't overly tall, about six feet even. Nor was he built like a football player. Rather, he seemed to be a creation of lean muscle and lithe sinew.

It was those eyes, she thought. That essence, that magnetism that made him so unique, so unusual, was in the way he looked at life. In the way he looked at a woman.

Amber wasn't sure why his gaze was so sensual. It was a look that seemed to dismiss a woman even as it assessed her. He could be so many things. Sometimes cordial, courteous, his manner flawless. And then other times, when they were alone, he could touch her, and it wouldn't matter who they were, or that she knew nothing about him. No, she knew something. She had known it from the beginning. He was dangerous. Everything about him hinted of the dark side....

Yet she could not deny his appeal. It was stronger than fear, and far stronger than reason.

There was something about Michael Adams....

Secret Service?

Perhaps. There were a number of politicians aboard. Presidential hopefuls, once the Old Man's term came to an end. The ship was probably crawling with bodyguards and Secret Service men. It was likely that he was among them.

And she had been glad of him—grateful, even, for such a deadly fascination, she realized. When three champagne cocktails could not stem the tide of her loneliness, she could seek him out and wonder about him. When she told herself that she had made an awful mistake, she would realize that it was possible to be interested in another man. No, not just interested. Much more than that. He wasn't a man to hold and to keep, not this one. For all his appeal, he was like rocket fuel, volatile, dangerous.

He was a sensual man. From the very first time she had seen him, she had felt his appeal. From the first time he had touched her, she had known it could not be denied. In his arms when they had danced she had felt the swift quickening of her heart. There was something raw and powerful about him. He was living on the edge—dangerous—but still he attracted her. He would attract any woman, she thought.

He was often near her...so where was he now?

Two black wraiths held Senator Ian Daldrin. And they weren't ignoring her anymore. They were staring at her, daring her to move. And she was frozen against the ship's railing, staring back at them, wondering how in God's name she could stop a kidnapping.

"Don't do it, I'm warning you!" she shouted.

They didn't release the senator. Instead, as she watched, someone slapped a cloth over his mouth, and Senator Daldrin fell into a man's waiting arms without a whimper. He was carried to the railing, then handed over.

"You'll never get away with this!" Amber screamed.

Two men still remained. They glanced at one another, as if making a decision about her, then started toward her. She had to do something. They had kidnapped the senator, and they meant to do something awful to her.

She wasn't armed in any way. In fact, she was barely dressed, she reflected ruefully. She was in a sheer white silk cocktail gown, her shoulders bare, a gauzy white scarf floating around her. It occurred to her that someone could snuff out her life in a few seconds by winding that scarf around her throat. She carried a tiny evening bag studded with little pearls, and wore sandals with four-inch heels.

Heels. That was it.

She slipped out of her shoes as they approached her, still shouting at them all the while, warning them, but growing more and more incoherent. It didn't matter what she was saying. She just wanted to be heard. She wanted Michael Adams to make an appearance and pull out a gun and save them all.

But it was unlikely that anyone would hear her, she thought, watching as they came closer. They weren't dressed in jeans and sweatshirts, she realized. They were dressed in wet suits. Wet suits and ski masks.

One of them murmured something to the other. Amber didn't recognize the language.

Her screams faded as she realized that the men were not empty-handed. They were carrying sharp-bladed knives that caught the slim glow of moonlight and shimmered like silver.

''No!'' she whispered.

They intended to kill her, she realized. They weren't going to kidnap her—they were going to kill her. When the first man reached for her, she began to scream again, however uselessly. She was caught and tossed to the deck, slammed hard against the boards. Desperately, she clawed at her attacker's face. Her nails caught at the ski mask, stripping it away.

Dark eyes stared at her. Deep set, in a slim swarthy face. Thin-lipped, taut. Amber inhaled desperately, then went limp, waiting for his hold to ease. When it did, she brought her knee up with all her strength. The man snarled and swore violently—in Spanish, she thought fleetingly. He raised his hand high, and again she saw the silver glimmer of his blade.

Her scream pierced the night as she waited for the knife to fall.

It did not.

Her attacker was suddenly wrenched away from her. Amber was so startled that she could barely move, barely breathe.

He was picked up by the scruff of his neck, then tossed roughly to the deck, where he landed with a thump against the ship's wooden railing.

A sharp spate of foreign oaths rang out, then Amber looked from her attacker to her rescuer, her sea-green eyes growing even larger.

It was Michael. He *had* been nearby, and he *had* come to her rescue, just as she had prayed.

He was standing with his feet apart, his hands on his hips, a look of cold blue fury in his eyes. He seemed to tower above the others, or maybe it was simply the force of his fury. He was in command, she thought, as disdainfully, with deadly venom, he chastised the man.

"Michael!" Amber whispered. She came up on her elbows, her hope-filled eyes on him, no hint of the truth registering in her mind yet.

He was in black jeans, black sneakers and a black turtleneck. There was a black knapsack on his back.

And he was speaking to the men who had attacked her, who had tried to kill her. Speaking in Spanish, then switching to another language.

Still, she refused to accept what she was seeing. She struggled to her feet, smoothing her long hair from her face, nervously looking at her rescuer.

"Michael . . . thank God!"

The second wraith in black started to laugh, moving toward her. Amber let out a frightened shriek and ran the few steps to Michael and threw herself into his arms.

He caught her, holding her shoulders stiffly, pushing her away. His eyes met hers, and she kept staring into them, denying the truth she saw there.

"No, Amber," he said softly. "No, I'm sorry. I'm not here to help you."

"You bastard."

The man in black murmured something, drawing patterns in the night air with his knife. Amber didn't understand a word of what he was saying, but his intentions were horribly obvious.

"Damn you, Amber, you should have run, you little fool!" Michael whispered to her.

She wrenched away from his touch and started to run as fast as she could.

Then she screamed, wrenched back by an implacable hold on her hair. She was slammed against a hard body and found herself staring up again into Michael's ice-fire eyes.

The man in black said something she didn't understand. She understood Michael's answer, though. It was a definite, razor sharp no.

"Let me go," Amber began to plead, but tears instantly stung her eyes and she screamed in pain as he tightened his grip on her hair. Then his free hand landed hard over her mouth, and she felt him whisper against her ear.

"Shut up, Miss Larkspur. Shut up. *Now.* I'm doing my best to save your miserable little interfering life!"

She didn't keep quiet to obey him; she did so because she was practically suffocating. He spoke harshly in a foreign language again. She thought it might be Arabic, but she wasn't certain. The man he had dragged off her rose, eyeing Michael warily as he did so. He stood beside the railing, apparently following instructions, and motioned to someone below. He was answered by a beam of light slashing through the darkness.

Michael Adams pulled Amber close against him again, whispering harshly, "This is my party, Miss Larkspur. You weren't invited, but you're here." His words didn't really matter, she thought, because any minute she was going to pass out. She couldn't speak; she could only inhale the scent of him.

Every man had a scent. Even freshly showered and shaved and wearing cologne, he had his own unique scent. She knew Michael Adams's. She knew it very well. She had lain beside him, and she had breathed in that scent again and again....

Again the sense of betrayal knifed into her. He had made love to her. He had touched her as no other man had touched her before, in ways that went beyond the senses and reached into the soul.

Now he was touching her again—and threatening her life.

She was probably about to die, she thought. Should her life be flashing before her eyes? She had lived a good life. An army brat, she'd grown up all over the world. And now she was part of the best of Washington society. She'd gone to the best schools, had the most fascinating opportunities. She'd learned what pain was, too. Losing her mother ten years ago had been anguish. And she'd learned about facing reality, because admitting that she could not change Peter had been like admitting she had wasted five years of her life, that dreams could never come true. She was young and privileged and well educated, and she had even been told that she was beautiful, but none of it had meant anything, because she had been unable to help Peter. She had finally let him go it on his own, and she had known that she would be okay when she had met Michael, when she had heard his whisper, felt his hands, his passion. In his arms she had learned how dearly, how sweetly, she loved life. . . .

She didn't want to die. She could beg; she could plead. She could ask him to remember what they had shared.

No. He was a traitor. She would never bow before him. She was her father's child. And if there was anything that Ted Larkspur's daughter had learned through the years, it was courage.

When Michael Adams began to release his hold on her mouth, Amber inhaled deeply, then screamed again.

"Damn you!" he swore, and for once his confident demeanor was ruffled. His fingers clamped over her mouth again in a punishing vise. "Stop it!" he hissed. "Amber, I'll give you one warning—"

She bit him. She sank her teeth into his index finger, but he didn't cry out. Instead, calmly, he hit her. The knuckles of his free hand came up and caught her jaw. It didn't seem so terribly hard. It didn't even seem really painful.

But her mind began to spin, and brilliant stars seemed to explode across the heavens. Then the stars faded, and she saw no more.

She awoke with a dull headache. Nothing of what had happened came to her at first; she was aware only of the sound of water lapping against the hull of a ship. She didn't open her eyes; she just listened to the sound of the water.

Then she became aware of voices. Men were speaking, arguing, in Spanish, she thought.

Her fingers curled into the cushions. These men would kill her without blinking an eye. It wouldn't matter that she was young, that she was a woman. They had come for the senator, and she had gotten in the way. But she was still alive. For how long, though?

Finally Amber opened her eyes, quickly closing them against the pain of the sudden light, then slowly opening them again.

She had surmised quickly that she was still at sea. Now she saw that she was on a couch in the salon area of a cabin cruiser.

It was probably about a sixty-footer, she thought, and a nice piece of workmanship at that. She was across from a large table where ten or twelve people could be comfortably seated for a meal. To her right was a galley, complete with a counter, refrigerator, stove, washer and dryer, and endless wood cabinets. There was a door to her right, leading to cabins, she assumed. She thought the vessel might easily sleep twelve or fourteen in comfort.

She slid her legs over the side of the couch. Her shoes were gone, and her stockings were torn and stained. She shivered. Her scarf was gone, too, and it was cold in the cabin. Her jaw was sore. She moved it carefully. Nothing seemed to be broken.

The men were still arguing.

Amber stood up carefully, stretching, gaining her balance. Perhaps she could find a life jacket and jump into the sea. She would rather take her chances with sharks than fanatics.

Where was the senator? she wondered sickly. Had they killed him already? Or had he been taken for ransom?

There was a scurry of noise from above. Amber sat down quickly, determined to pretend that she was asleep. But she was too late. The man whose mask she had stripped away was hurrying down a short flight of stairs into the galley. He met her eyes and smiled.

She realized then that he spoke English, at least one word of it. "Up," he told her.

He reached to touch her, and she moved quickly. "I'm up."

She stood up again, but he touched her anyway, pushing her ahead of him. They came to the little flight of steps, and he shoved her forward. She pushed open a half-closed doorway and nearly stumbled over the step that led to the outer deck, still cloaked in night's darkness.

High above her head was the helm, covered by a canopy. Before her, lounging in an assortment of deck chairs, was an array of men. She hadn't been uncon-

scious very long, she determined. Several of them were
still clad in wet suits.

There was a swarthy older man there, cloaked in a
burnoose from head to toe. He gave Michael his full
attention, as did the five younger men—subordi-
nates, or so it seemed.

Michael was leaning against the rail. When Amber
appeared, barefoot and indignant, her chin high while
her heart trembled, he allowed his gaze to sweep over
her, but his attention remained on the older man. He
spoke slowly in Spanish—switching into another language on occasion to press a point.

The man behind Amber exploded in fury. Then
Michael spoke a sentence in English, insistently.

"She is my concern. Mine."

A spate of Spanish broke out again.

Michael interrupted sharply, speaking briefly before he gave a harsh laugh, which all the men shared.

"What the hell is going on?" Amber demanded,
narrowing her eyes. Maybe they were trying to decide
whether to just throw her overboard or slit her throat
and *then* throw her overboard. She was certain that at
least half of these men wanted her dead. "None of you
has any rights where I'm concerned! You're criminals! You let me go—and the senator—this instant or
I swear I shall—"

Michael interrupted her, turning from her as he
spoke to the older man as if nothing she said mattered, as if she hadn't even spoken. He kept speaking
to the older man—the only other man whose opinion
seemed to count.

"Where is the senator?" Amber demanded.

They all stopped then, staring at her.

"Shut up," Michael Adams told her flatly.

She couldn't let him turn away again. They were probably going to kill her one way or the other, so it really didn't matter what she said anymore.

"They'll hang you, Michael Adams. They'll get you, you bastard, one way or the other. Maybe they'll shoot you for treason. It's a pity they don't draw and quarter men anymore. It would be a fitting way for you to go."

His ice-blue eyes fell on her with complete disdain. "Shut up, Amber."

"The hell I will—" she began.

Three quick strides brought him to her before she could even attempt to back away. He struck her again, open-handed, his palm cracking loudly against her cheek. Tears rose instantly to her eyes, and she tasted blood where her teeth had caught the vulnerable flesh of her inner lip. She swore silently that she would not go down without a fight, that she would not be a pathetic victim, refusing to battle. She struck him with swift venom, startling him when her fingers connected with his face.

A roar of laughter went up.

Someone shouted out to Michael, and the sentence contained a word she understood. *Puta.* Whore. They were calling her Michael's whore, she realized, and laughing because the man who held sway over all of them didn't seem to be able to handle his whore. They all wanted to have something on him, she realized. They were afraid of him.

At the moment she was afraid of him herself. She forgot that his intervention had saved her life. That it was still the only thing standing between her and death.

"No!" she shrilled furiously. "I am nothing to this man! Listen to me—"

"Shut up!" Michael ground out savagely. He grabbed her, wrenching her off her feet, and tossed her over his shoulder. His voice rose with rage, and he snapped out something in Spanish.

There was laughter again. They weren't laughing at Michael anymore; they were laughing at her.

Michael kicked open the door and started down the steps that had brought her to the deck. Gasping, Amber saw that they were passing through the galley and the salon where she had so recently lain.

She had been afraid of death; she had never even thought about rape. Now the echo of coarse male laughter reached her, and a new terror was born within her soul.

They slammed through a hallway, then into a tiny hot cabin where the only illumination came from a pale ray of moonlight.

Amber was cast like refuse upon a narrow bunk. For a moment she lay stunned; then she twisted in panic, her heart racing. She started to rise, but she was caught and thrown back.

She couldn't really see Michael in the humid darkness. All she could see was a silhouette, dark and menacing.

Then she heard a rustle in the darkness, and the silhouette of the man began to glow. He had shed the black turtleneck, and the rippling muscles of his chest were gleaming in the pale light.

She stared at him, able to see his eyes at last, the fathomless blue-ice eyes that had once so fascinated her.

"Let me go, you son of a bitch!" she grated, her voice shaking with vehemence.

He looked at her without emotion, without deigning to reply. He unbuckled his belt, and it slipped from the loops of his jeans with a curious slithering sound. Amber's eyes widened as she saw him wrap the leather around his hand and wield the length of it like a whip. Dear God, he meant to beat her into silence.

She let out a long scream of horrified anticipation. The leather made a snakelike hissing sound as it rent the air and struck . . . the bedding, not her flesh.

Perhaps she was in shock. Amber couldn't grasp what was happening. Half gasping, half laughing and very near tears, she stared at him. "Dear God. Oh God . . ."

He took a step toward the bunk so that he could whisper in the night. She saw the white flash of his teeth and the deadly warning in his eyes. "Scream again."

"What?"

"Scream again."

"Michael, I don't—"

"You idiot. I said *scream*!"

His eyes met hers for a second, then fell to the white bodice of her gown. He released her shoulders and bluntly reached for the fabric between her breasts, then wrenched it apart.

Amber clawed at his hands, screaming. "Don't! Don't!" Hysteria was rising within her. Not this. Not this, not from him . . .

He smiled, his teeth flashing again. There seemed to be a touch of humor in his eyes. "Good scream," he told her, and then he proceeded to rip the bodice of her white cocktail gown until it was split to her navel.

He wanted screams, she gave him a barrage of them, clawing at his hands, his face, his throat, pummeling anything she could reach.

"Good," he murmured to her, releasing her suddenly. Amber fell against the wall, struggling to hold her clothing together, gasping for breath and completely dazed.

Michael Adams sat at the foot of the bed, untied his black sneakers and tossed them across the cabin.

"I'll kill you myself!" Amber swore, close to tears, fighting them wildly.

He reached behind him to his waistband and produced a smooth steel weapon, then set it on a bureau by the bed. Amber caught her breath, gazing at the gun longingly.

Then her eyes darted back to him. He was standing again, sliding out of the black jeans, and moonlight was dancing over the whole of his body.

He had worn nothing beneath the jeans.

"No!"

This time he replied, chuckling softly. "Amber, my love, there's nothing new here...."

The deep husky tone of his voice nearly demolished the last of her sanity. How dare he remind her of how familiar they were to one another?

He let out a very explicit oath, then fell on top of her. She felt his flesh against her body. Her white gown fell open, and the rough hair on his chest brushed over her breasts. A scream rose in her throat again, but she didn't let it loose. His eyes were on her, piercing into her own. He brought his hand up and softly stroked her cheek. "You fool. For God's sake, give yourself a chance."

He was going to kill her now, she thought. She could fight, but she couldn't win.

She moistened her lips. "Don't..." she whispered. She kept her eyes on his. Maybe there was mercy somewhere within him.

"Listen to me. And listen good. I am trying to keep you alive."

She nodded. Sure. Sure he was.

He moved away, sitting at the foot of the bunk, running his fingers through his hair. He seemed to have forgotten her, but then she must have moved, or breathed, or something, and she drew his attention again.

He looked at her torn bodice and her breasts and her skirt bunched up beneath her hips. "Take that off," he told her.

"No, Michael. No, I—"

He rose, leaning over her. "Now. You can do it, or I can. If I do it, it's going to be worse."

"If they don't shoot you, I swear that *I* will!" Amber vowed, desperately fighting against hands that moved with a steely will. The grim line of his mouth tightened, but other than that he gave no indication that he had even heard her.

Then she tried to grab the gun, and he could no longer ignore her. Calmly, forcefully, coldly, with grim determination, he stripped away her clothing.

Any struggle was useless. Her once glorious gown was shredded, and he didn't stop there. Without any finesse he stripped off her stockings and slip, then unsnapped her bra. He leaned closer to her, whispering in her ear. "Damn it, I am not trying to hurt you! But if you keep trying to hurt me, so help me, I'll—"

He stopped speaking abruptly and walked to the door, naked in the darkness. His head was cocked, and he seemed to be listening.

She dissolved into silent tears when he lowered himself to the bed again. When he spoke, his voice was a soft whisper that was curiously tender, almost a caress.

"Get under the blanket and move over. Quickly."

"No—"

"Before God, Miss Larkspur, do it!"

Miss Larkspur. As if there was still something formal left in their relationship.

He grabbed the blanket, tossing it over her. Then he crawled in beside her, lacing his fingers behind his head and staring up at the ceiling of the small cabin.

Amber didn't dare breathe. He seemed to be listening again. She listened, too. She could hear men talking, occasionally laughing.

Michael turned to her suddenly, fiercely, in the darkness. "One warning, Miss Larkspur, don't play me for a fool. You're supposed to be an intelligent woman. Prove it. Whatever I say, do. Whatever game I play, you play along. Understand?"

Her tears were subsiding, but her breath still came in ragged gasps. She nodded.

He stared into her eyes, compassion touching his, filling them with a curious warmth. "I'm trying to help you. Do you understand?"

"Of course," Amber managed to whisper coolly. Help her. Sure. Strip her, humiliate her.

"I'm sorry. I'm sorry you got involved."

"You're a traitor, you bastard!" she hissed, trembling.

She felt him stiffen; then his hand wound around her wrist, and she nearly winced from the pain. "What I am doesn't matter, Amber. Not if you want to survive this."

She lay silent, aching. She didn't want him to be a bad guy. She didn't want to believe that he would kill her, that he would kill others. And his touch upon her was too forceful for her to speak against him again. Courage had its limits. He was lying too close to her, his body nearly touching hers. She could feel his warmth, and she was painfully aware of the length of him nearly touching her from head to toe.

"Listen to me, Amber. You must."

She was silent, staring at him.

"Get some sleep," he told her, then turned away, offering her his back.

Get some sleep, he had told her. As if she could. A sob escaped her, a sob she quickly swallowed. Then she bit the back of her hand to keep from crying all over again.

From somewhere, from the bureau perhaps, she heard the ticking of a clock. Then he whispered to her again. "It's going to be all right. I promise you, it will be all right."

He touched her cheek. She shoved his hand away, biting her lower lip for courage. "Fine. So you say. Just—just don't touch me."

"I'll do my best . . . Miss Larkspur."

She felt him watching her, and she thought how absurd the situation was. They were lying naked together, under the same blanket. He had just kidnapped her and a United States senator right off a cruise ship.

He turned his back on her again, but it was a small bunk and when his body brushed hers, she trembled. She couldn't help feeling that it should be all right, that she was secure beside him again, something archaic and pagan, as if he was the mate who could look after her through the darkness of the night.

She heard the clock again, ticking out the night.

Amber felt the man beside her, and she prayed for morning to come.

She hated him, but he had saved her. This man was all that stood between her and the others, she realized.

And then she stopped praying so fervently for morning's light. She hoped that the night would go on forever.

Washington, D.C.
June 16, 8:30 a.m.

It was morning before the news reached the White House. And it was Ben Hurley who first received word, rather than Ted Larkspur. It was about to hit the media, so Ben hurriedly went to the president, who summoned Ted.

"It went off as expected. They got Ian. Adams was there, and he disappeared, too."

Ted swallowed and nodded. Now they had to wait.

Ben cleared his throat. "Uh, Ted . . ."

Surprised, Ted Larkspur looked at Hurley, who cleared his throat again.

"Amber has disappeared, too."

Ted Larkspur blanched. "What? What do you mean, disappeared? She's in Palm Beach with friends—"

Ben shook his head unhappily. "We just heard it from the ship's captain. Amber was aboard the *Alexandria*. She boarded the ship in Miami."

"Knowing Amber," the president said softly, "she probably wrote to tell you—"

Ted groaned. He hadn't been home. She'd tried to call him at work. He'd meant to get back to her. He'd been so busy and so worried and now...

Now, because of his involvement, Amber was involved, too. The *Alexandria*! He could have warned her. He could have told her not to go. He could have done something, even if he had lied and said that he was ill, and that she had to come right home....

He gripped the desk and he tried to stand, but he started to fall anyway.

The president leaped to his feet. Together, he and Hurley got Ted into the presidential chair.

"Oh, my God!" Ted breathed. He was going to start crying. He was an old army man, and he was going to start crying.

Ben Hurley cleared his throat yet again. The president began to talk. He was a good soother; he'd had practice.

"It's bad, Ted. Yes, it's bad. But Tchartoff is there. Tchartoff isn't the type to let anything happen to her."

"What can he do?" Ted asked dully. His only child. His beautiful daughter, his little girl, had been taken.

"He'll do something. I know it. Tchartoff will do something."

Ted didn't want to hear the name.

This was his own fault. It was all his own fault. He should have buried the dossier.

He leaned back in the chair. Was it only a month ago that he had first brought Adam Tchartoff—alias Michael Adams—to Washington? One short month ago....

Chapter 1

Washington, D.C.
May 15

Sir?"

Ted Larkspur stood just inside the French doors, the dossier he carried held behind his back, his legs spread at ease. He was quite comfortable with the position; he was a retired military man who'd somehow found himself working on Capitol Hill. He was still a young man—at least, far younger than the chief executive.

The president was down on the floor, giving his attention to a jigsaw puzzle. From what Ted could make out, the picture was a Western scene.

The president looked up with a slightly absent smile, greeted Ted cordially, then looked at the puzzle again. Ted wasn't deceived; he knew he had the man's attention.

"You've got something for me?"

"Yes, sir. I think I've got exactly what you want."

The president reached out, and Ted stepped forward to hand him the folder, taking care not to tramp on the puzzle.

Still on the floor, the president opened the file. Dark eyes surrounded by the creases of many decades quickly scanned the report. He stared for a long time at the eight-by-ten glossy of a man he found in the file.

The face was an interesting one. Full of contradictions. Close-cropped light hair, light eyes—the color was impossible to tell from the black-and-white photo. Broad cheekbones, yet the face was still somehow slim. The nose had been broken somewhere along the line. The mouth was full, but held tightly. The standard glossy caught something of the man behind the face. Something of a sharp stare. Something keen, alert. Wary. Not so much as if he was always watching, but as if he was always . . . prepared.

"Fascinating," the president said.

He set the dossier by his feet and picked up a piece of the puzzle.

Ted Larkspur cleared his throat. "I believe, sir, the piece you're holding goes up higher. It's not grass—it's sky, where the sun's rays start."

"I believe you're right, Larkspur."

He sighed with satisfaction as the piece fell into position. Then his gaze met Larkspur's again, and Ted shivered a little; there hadn't been a second during the interchange when the president had really forgotten his purpose.

"We have to do something, Ted."

Ted didn't reply. The president didn't really want an answer.

Once again the president gave his attention to the puzzle. "This man—this Adam Tchartoff—his citizenship is Israeli now?"

"Yes, sir."

"But he was an American?"

"Yes, sir. It's all in the dossier there—"

"I got what I wanted from the dossier. The rest I want from you. You've seen him."

"Briefly. We weren't introduced."

"But you've seen him, Ted." The president tapped the dossier at his feet with a puzzle piece. "Don't ever let anyone fool you, Ted. This paper—pulp—with some neat facts and figures in ink. You never know a man until you've seen him."

"Yes, sir," Ted agreed.

"So." The president started to rise. Ted moved forward to help him, but the older man waved him away. "I can still rise on my own power, boy." He walked behind his desk and sat, folding his hands prayer fashion and leaning his head against the back of the chair as he stared at the ceiling.

"Why do you suppose he gave up his U.S. citizenship, Ted?"

"I, uh, don't really know, sir," Ted offered.

The president shifted and tapped a pencil on his desk. "Born in Linz, Austria, in 1950 of a White Russian refugee and a Polish Jewess. But the Austrians weren't giving refugee infants citizenship in those days.''

Ted was surprised that the man had read so much in the few seconds his eyes had flicked over the file.

"That's right, sir. His parents moved to the United States in 1954—he acquired his citizenship a few years later. His father died in 1967—that's when he moved to Israel with his mother."

"But he didn't change his citizenship right away," the president mused. He lifted a brow. "He let us draft him into the U.S. Army first."

Ted shrugged.

The president continued. "He served out his time in 'Nam, then he became an Israeli. What do you think of that?"

"Well, begging your pardon, sir, there's really not much for a man to do once he comes home, after he's been in the Special Services. I mean, you spend weeks, months, years, learning to be a savage—" Ted broke off.

The president laughed dryly. "Yes, I see your point. It's hard to come home to a suit and tie and Wall Street." His fingers drummed against the desk. "But he wasn't a violent man. He was an accountant."

"For several years, sir. He was asked by his government to work in a...new capacity about five years ago. They needed his expertise for a rather tricky situation."

The president looked at Ted sharply. "That's when his alias was created?"

"Yes."

"When were his wife and child killed?"

"Two years ago. A car bomb went off when they were at the seashore on vacation. His name had become known. His wife and child were inside—he had gotten out to buy a pack of cigarettes."

"It's a shame. A real shame."

"Yes, it is."

The president exhaled, staring at his puzzle. "But now, for our purposes . . . you're sure he can't be recognized?"

"He's always worked undercover. No one would recognize him since the car bombing. To the world at large he's a completely harmless bureaucrat. On the other hand, in certain circles, the alias, Michael Adams, is legendary. His reputation under that name allowed him to infiltrate the Death Squad without any difficulty. The Israeli connection is completely unknown."

"I'm not sure I understand."

"The persona was created slowly and carefully. Events, assassinations were all laid at his feet. The Death Squad is quite a conglomeration, you know. Dissatisfied Central and South Americans, and then a hard-core group from a number of the Arabic countries. They train in North Africa—we know that. Codes are usually in Spanish—but sometimes in Arabic. Once Adam tried to infiltrate as Michael Adams, the group pounced right on him."

"Tell me more about Tchartoff."

"He first went to Israel to see his mother, then he stayed for his wife." Ted hesitated, then added softly, "Then, I think, he stayed for revenge."

The president gazed at his desk, his fingers drumming on it. "So he's still angry..."

"Bitterly angry. That kind of loss is a pain that doesn't go away."

The drumming ceased as the older man stared at Ted abruptly. "I think he's perfect. Can you arrange a meeting? Not in Washington, of course. The United States government is going to have nothing to do with this, you understand."

"I understand your position perfectly, sir. No information of any kind will be on file. No one will know anything about it, except those directly involved, and they'll know only what they're told."

"I want our men back. I want that ring of cutthroats busted sky-high. I do not want a pack of mercenary terrorists calling the shots in this country, and I don't want them getting off in any foreign court."

"No, sir," Ted agreed. He hesitated a moment. "He's in Washington now. I called him about a ceremony to honor his old unit. He should have come in just about—" he paused to look at his watch "—an hour ago."

The president glanced at Ted with some surprise, then he smiled with slow and rueful admiration. "When is the ceremony?"

"Tomorrow at two."

"I assume that my schedule is free, and that I'll be able to attend?"

"Yes. You'll be able to observe Mr. Tchartoff before you meet with him."

The president nodded, satisfied. "Let's just hope, shall we, that he's still angry enough to accept our bait. Does he know our latest intelligence?"

"That the Death Squad was responsible for the bomb that killed his wife?"

"Yes."

"I don't know. He may have suspected."

"But we have proof." The president sat back. "I'm looking forward to meeting Mr. Tchartoff." He smiled. "I hear that someone else is due in today."

Ted felt a wide grin form. "Yes." He glanced at his watch. "Amber should have arrived this morning. She said that she wanted to explore the Smithsonian, then she would come to lunch."

"I'd like to see her. Can the two of you come to dinner this evening?"

"I'm sure that Amber will be delighted."

"Good."

Amber Larkspur stared at the giant elephant in the center of the rotunda of the Museum of Natural History. As many times as she had come here, she still loved the place. Just as she loved the Museum of the American People and the art museums and the Air and Space Museum and everything else about the entire Smithsonian Institution.

There was no place quite like Washington, D.C. She had missed it.

A group of schoolchildren came running out of the hallway leading to the sea creatures. Laughing, they raced for the elephant.

Amber carefully stepped out of their way, smiling. As an army brat, she'd done a lot of moving around. But what time she had spent in one place had been here—or, really, Alexandria, Virginia. As a kid she had come on field trips here, just as these kids were doing now. Life had been so simple then—and, of course, she hadn't had the good sense to appreciate it. Not the simplicity, not the beauty. She smiled to herself, remembering the old saying—youth was wasted on the young.

Not that she was old, she reminded herself. But she had just turned twenty-nine, and she couldn't deny that it was knowing thirty was just around the corner that had made her change her life so drastically last week.

A young couple looking around a little bit helplessly caught Amber's attention. She smiled, realizing that they wanted to be together in a picture. She stepped forward, offering to snap a shot for them.

"Oh, will you?" The young woman, a pretty little brunette, flushed. "Thank you so much. This is our honeymoon, and we haven't got a single picture together so far."

"What a shame!" Amber said, smiling. "You should just ask. People here are great. Honestly. They'll be happy to help you."

She took a few pictures for them, then glanced at her watch. She wasn't due to meet her father for a half hour yet. Not enough time to see another museum, but too much time for hurrying.

The couple thanked her, then asked her advice on the city. She suggested an itinerary for them, then saw them off with a wave.

Babies, she thought. Neither one of them could be over twenty. And they were married and off on a honeymoon. Just like playing house, only it was the real world.

Amber stepped outside. May was such a beautiful month here. The sky was mostly clear, with only a soft puff of cloud visible here and there. The cherry blossoms were out, the grass was green, and the world was beautiful.

She stuck her hands into the pockets of her blazer, crossed the street and idly began to wander along the grass toward the subway station. It felt like summer was here; even on a workday, it was evident. A young man tossed a Frisbee to a dog. Two women—office workers, perhaps, judging by their fashionable dresses—picnicked on the lawn. There was a softball game going on about a hundred yards away. All around her she could hear laughter, and it was nice.

"This is the world," she murmured to herself. "All you have to do is open the door and step into it."

She smiled and picked up the tempo of her walk, her shoulder bag swinging beside her. She passed by a park bench with a man sitting on it.

She didn't know why, but when she had passed the man, she turned back to look at him.

He was just sitting there. He looked like a million other men on a warm day in the park. He was wearing jeans, sneakers and a denim shirt. His arms were stretched out along the back of the bench, and his face was turned to the sun, as if he was savoring the warmth.

Even as she stared at him, he looked up, staring straight at her in return. It was uncanny. He had sensed her. She wasn't moving, she hadn't uttered a word, but he had known that she was watching him, and he had known exactly where she was standing.

She flushed, but though she meant to, she didn't draw her eyes away from his immediately. He was too intriguing. She couldn't begin to judge his age, except that he was still young enough—though young enough for what, she wasn't sure. He wasn't handsome; he was arresting. His features were rugged and strong, his eyes mesmerizing. They were light, she thought. She couldn't really see them, but they were light, and he was reading her quickly, like an open book, instantly storing away whatever he saw, whatever he thought. There was a brooding intensity about him, she thought. An energy that lingered beneath his pose of lethargy.

Then he smiled. It wasn't a lascivious smile—not the type of smile she might have expected from a strange man who had caught her staring at him in the park. It was just an interested smile, and maybe a slightly amused one. If he didn't smile, she thought, he might be the type of man to make a person tremble. He wasn't a man she would want to cross.

"Hello," he said.

Amber felt a little like a fool. She nodded, then smiled in return. He was an intriguing man, but Washington was full of them. Powerful men, ambitious men. She felt that this one was powerful, but maybe not so ambitious. Or maybe he just didn't have the same ambitions as other men. It didn't matter, she assured herself. She was standing there staring at him, which was rude, and the least she could do was say hello back.

"Hello," she returned. Then she swung around quickly and started for the subway station. As she walked, she felt that he was still looking at her. She turned around. He *was* watching her. And he didn't pretend to look elsewhere when she caught him; in fact, he waved. She waved back, then kept walking, more quickly. She even ran down the steps when she reached the subway.

Once she was seated on the train, she tried to think ahead to lunch with her father, but the face of the stranger kept coming back to her.

It would fade, she assured herself.

By the time she reached the restaurant, she had almost forgotten his face. She wanted to tell her father the truth about what she was doing. She didn't want him to feel sorry for her—she didn't want him to say, "I told you so," and she didn't want him to worry. But neither could she forget five years of her life, and she didn't want to pretend that what she was going through wasn't heartbreaking.

They had arranged to meet at Zefferelli's, a hole-in-the-wall not too far from the Capitol building. Amber arrived first. She was pleased when Zefferelli recognized her and led her to a small booth in the back with a single glowing candle and a spotless white cloth. Amber ordered wine, then sat back to wait for her father.

He arrived within five minutes. She saw him enter and speak with Zefferelli. She jumped to her feet, waving. She was so proud of him. He was a handsome man, with a distinguished touch of gray at the temples and his lean, straight form. He meant everything in the world to her, now more than ever.

He weaved his way among the tables and came over to her. She hugged him enthusiastically, curiously near crying as she did. She laughed, and her eyes watered, and they broke apart at last and sat across from one another.

After they ordered, Amber began by asking him about life in the White House. He told her about the president's granddaughter, an eighteen-month-old, who had been left with the goldfish for a moment. She had taken all the pretty little creatures out and laid them on the table. The poor baby had been heartbroken to discover that they had all died.

Amber laughed; then Ted told her with a sigh that things weren't going very well. They'd had another diplomat kidnapped in Rome the other day.

"How terrible!" Amber cried softly. "Did he have a family?"

Her father swallowed a sip of water. "Two little girls, a young, pretty wife."

"It makes my problems seem rather shallow," she murmured.

Ted Larkspur took his daughter's hands in his own. "Nothing about you has ever been shallow, sweetheart. What's going on? I've been worried sick since you called."

"I left Peter, Dad."

Ted absorbed the information silently, nodding. "For good?"

She shrugged. "Maybe I didn't really intend to at first. I don't know. Maybe I was dreaming. I might have thought that if I actually walked away—packed my bags, stored my belongings—he would realize that I wasn't bluffing." She smiled ruefully, picking up her wineglass. "We all just keep on believing in Prince Charming, I suppose. I thought he'd run after me and swear that he understood. So far, it hasn't happened."

Ted looked at Amber. He didn't want to say, "I told you so," but his values had been right in this case.

"Maybe you never should have moved in with him."

Amber smiled. She had been expecting this. "Dad, I still believe that a forced marriage would have been a far worse thing." She laughed. "But marriage wasn't the point. It's my age, I think. It's the old biological clock. I'm almost thirty."

Ted smiled. She might have been mentioning the fact that she was coming up on her centennial.

"I do believe that Peter loves you. I don't think I could ever have endured that living arrangement if I didn't believe that. Do you think he'll come after you?"

Amber thought about the night—just two nights ago—when she had walked out of her home of five years. Over the past two years she had contemplated the move. Peter didn't want marriage; he didn't want to raise a family. He did love her, and more: he needed her.

He was five years older than she was, a good-looking man with dark hair and bright Irish eyes, a deep barrel chest, dimples and an easy smile. She'd fallen for him the moment they had met—in a bowling alley. He'd been seeing someone else at the time, and she had lain awake night after night praying that he would eventually call her.

He did. Casual dates at first—she knew that he was still seeing the other woman. She had refused to enter into a sexual relationship with him until she was the only one in his life. She was far from world-weary at twenty-five, but she knew that if she began a relationship that way, it would never change.

She should have been savvy enough to realize that the same thing applied to their living arrangements. Peter was a sweetheart. He was charming, and he would do anything for her—except make a complete commitment and agree to children. He loved her, he needed her, but he really had to keep thinking about children.

Well, he had been thinking for years.

Amber smiled sadly. He still didn't believe that she was really gone, she was sure. She loved Peter, but she wanted children, and she didn't believe in tricking any man into something that he didn't want. Children deserved to be loved and wanted—by both parents.

She didn't want a place to live—she wanted a home. She wanted a big backyard with some ridiculously huge German shepherd to slobber all over them. It didn't seem like so much to ask out of life. All her friends envied her, she knew. She was well traveled, well educated; her father was a key man at the White House; she and Peter both made good money.

She had everything. Except for kids. Except for a simple gold band around her finger.

"Amber?"

"I'm sorry, Dad. I was wandering, I suppose."

"I said, do you think he'll come after you?"

"I don't know. Maybe. But I'm already wondering if it would be enough."

Zefferelli came over with their tortellini. Amber told her father that she had resigned from the magazine where she had been an associate editor. Ted remained silent as she told him that she planned to take some time off, then see if she could get a job with one of the Washington papers.

"It will work out," he told his daughter.

She smiled, and he wondered how any man could let a woman escape when she had a smile like that and a heart the size of Kansas. And a mane of hair like a lioness, blue-green eyes like the Caribbean and a slim, shapely form to rival any man's fantasy.

He was prejudiced, of course. He was her father. He would have liked to drag Peter Greenborough to the altar with a shotgun. But that wasn't what she wanted, and he knew it. Well, it was her life.

"By the way, the president has asked us to dinner."

"How nice!" Amber exclaimed. She was lying. She didn't want to go to dinner at the White House. They wouldn't be alone. There would be senators, other politicians. They would pair her off with some eligible man, and she would be miserable all night.

One way or the other, she would be miserable. But at the moment she just wanted to be miserable alone. She wanted to imagine Peter's face and dream that he would come for her, ready to convince her that he couldn't go on without a real commitment, either. That he was dying for children. Twins, triplets...

Amber paused suddenly, frowning. She wasn't imagining Peter's face, not the face she loved, not the face she had just left behind.

Curiously, she was seeing a stranger's piercing light eyes. The man on the park bench. The stranger with the rough but appealing face. The man who had frightened her, in a way...

And then compelled her on some different level.

She ate her tortellini. Was it better to imagine a stranger and shiver? Or think about Peter and suffer differently?

Maybe it was better to think about the man she would never see again. She could create all kinds of fantasies about him.

"I think I'll wander through Old Town Alexandria tomorrow," she told her father. "Want to come?"

He shook his head, feeling a tightening in his throat. "I—I have to go to a memorial service tomorrow."

"For what?"

"A unit that served in Vietnam."

"Oh. Forget Alexandria, Dad. I'm coming with you tomorrow."

A chill seized Ted. "It isn't necessary. It's just a small thing."

"No. Nothing like that is ever small. I want to come."

Ted looked at her, then nodded. "Of course. Are you going to stay with me at the town house?"

He kept a small place near the Capitol and had a larger home in Alexandria. Amber started to shake her head. She had wanted to be alone. But she saw the eager expression in his eyes, and she told him, "I left my things in Alexandria. But I'll pick them up and come into the city."

He smiled, and Amber thought that, if nothing else, she would make him happy. And that was important to her. Very important.

Dinner that night was very much what she had expected. She was seated between an Arabian oil magnate and a French diplomat. Her French was good, but she didn't understand a word of Arabic. It didn't matter; both men spoke English perfectly, and both were charming.

During the meal Amber found herself looking to the head of the table, at the president. He was a wise old man, she thought, a country man come to the city—come to the world. He caught her gaze on him and winked.

Everything except politics was discussed at dinner. She spoke about the theater with the Arab, and new fashion trends with the Frenchman. Her father whispered to her warningly that both men were finding her charming and devastating. He claimed to be afraid that she would have a marriage offer that very night. The Arab gentleman already had two wives, but he was allowed four, so there was plenty of room in the tent for her.

Amber laughed. Later, she danced in the garden. There were a number of her father's old friends there, and some of her own. In the end, the evening was more enjoyable than she'd expected.

"Where is that Texan of yours tonight, Amber?" her friend Myra asked.

"He of the gorgeous biceps," Josie, another friend, teased.

"We've split up," Amber said lightly.

"Ah, a woman on her own," Josie said sagely.

"On her own? Well, then, she just has to come with us!" Myra insisted.

"Come where?" Amber asked.

"On vacation. We've arranged a trip to Florida. Palm Beach. What do you think?"

"You must come!" Josie added.

"I don't know..."

Peter might come for her. Was she really ready to be strong against him?

Florida . . . Maybe that was just what she needed.

"I'll think about it," Amber said.

"I'll call you with the details tomorrow," Josie told her.

"Fine," Amber said. "I'll look forward to hearing from you."

The Vietnam Memorial, Washington, D.C.
May 16

It was a beautiful, warm day. The sun shone overhead; the breeze was light.

There was quite a turnout for the ceremony. Sergeant Culpepper spoke eloquently about the men of the division, a Green Beret unit, more than seventy percent of whom had been left behind on foreign soil. There were tears among the friends and relatives who had come to remember. Amber felt the hot pressure of tears sting her eyes as she thought of the men who had fought in what was sometimes a forgotten war—not a war at all, as Sergeant Culpepper so eloquently reminded them, but a police action.

The media were all there, for the president was making an appearance. That meant security, of course. And Amber, being with her father, who was with the president, could scarcely turn around without being swamped by a sea of men in their perpetual blue suits.

The chaplain began the Lord's Prayer.

Amber folded her hands and looked down at the earth, then across the dais to where the chaplain was speaking.

She started violently, almost crying out.

The man from the park bench was there. The man with the curious ice-blue eyes. And he was staring straight at her.

He didn't look away. He continued to watch her, and she couldn't begin to imagine what he was thinking. She felt a shivering begin all along her spine. Who the hell was he?

She decided that she would be direct about the situation. When the ceremony was over, she would ask him. He must be a vet—a member of this unit, she imagined. He wasn't in uniform, though. He was wearing tan cotton slacks and a white tailored shirt, open at the collar. He was very bronze, like a man who spent a lot of time in the sun. His face was rugged because it was weathered, and intriguing because it spoke of character. He was handsome, but more because of his magnetism than his physical features. He seemed charged with a certain energy, with a sexuality that was dangerous and exciting and as tempting to a woman's curiosity as a flame was to a moth. She couldn't take her eyes off him.

The service was over. A cool breeze touched her face and lifted her hair. It was over, and she hadn't even realized that it had ended. She had been staring at the stranger from the park.

She meant to walk over to him. To introduce herself. It seemed like the most logical—and courteous—thing to do.

She started to walk toward him, but her father stopped her, catching her elbow, and began to speak to her.

By the time Amber turned around, the stranger was gone.

The crowd had begun to thin out with the president gone; dozens of the people present must have been from the Secret Service. Amber looked around for her father. He hadn't left with the president, she was certain. He wouldn't have left without saying goodbye.

She looked around. He was talking to someone; his graying head was bent over. Then he turned, walking away, his features caught in grim lines.

He had been talking with the man with the blue-ice eyes.

When he saw her, Ted Larkspur's face changed entirely. He smiled, but it was a false smile, as if he had donned a mask.

"Dad!"

"Sweetheart. Want another lunch with the old man? I have about two hours before duty calls again."

"Sure. I'd love lunch. Who was that?"

"Who was who?" he asked. She could tell he was being evasive.

"The man you were talking to. The one with the intriguing face and the blue eyes."

Ted waved a hand in the air. "I don't know. I spoke with a lot of people."

Amber thought it was curious that anyone could forget the stranger, but her father seemed worn and very tired. "Let's go to the town house. I'll make lunch."

"No, I'll buy you lunch."

"I'll make it," Amber insisted. She took his hand, and they walked to the curb. Today there would be no cabs. A government car was waiting.

Amber made omelets. Ted praised the food effusively, but he ate very little, then stood and kissed her. "I've got to go." He hesitated. "Are you all right?"

"Of course." She smiled, then searched his eyes. "Are you all right?"

"Of course."

He kissed her again, then he was gone.

Amber didn't want to sit around alone. She decided to take a nap, since she hadn't been sleeping well. But she only dozed, dreaming about the good times, about Peter coming in with a special bottle of wine, about the way they had learned to cook lamb together.

Curiously, the stranger's face kept intruding on her memories. He would appear at the most inappropriate times, like when she dreamed of walking out of a shower soaking wet and crawling into bed. Suddenly she would see his face and remember the way his bronzed flesh had looked against the casual white cotton of his shirt.

She got up and called Josie's number, determined that it would be a very good idea to spend a little time on the Florida sand.

Chapter 2

The President's Estate
Northern Virginia
May 16

At 6:30 that evening, a helicopter set down on the green expanse of lawn at a large country estate in northern Virginia.

The president was standing as Adam Tchartoff alighted from the chopper. Ted Larkspur watched the president and smiled pleasantly at his own secret thoughts as he watched the man duck slightly against the whirling wind caused by the blades.

The president assessed the man. He wasn't tall for a hero. No more than an even six feet. But he was quick, assured.

Faces, the president reminded himself. Words were

nothing but ink on paper. A face was the true measure of a man.

And he liked this man's face. It was intelligent. Hardened by life. It had a nice rugged appearance to it. Tchartoff wasn't going to win any beauty contests. His eyes were blue. Crystal blue, and as smooth and cutting and cold as ice. Yes, definitely an interesting, arresting face. A mouth that might have been sensitive at one time, but was a little grim now. He was tanned, not so much like a man who enjoyed sports but like a man who had lived constantly in the sun.

Tchartoff was dressed in a blue denim shirt and slightly worn jeans; true, he hadn't known where he was going or who he would be meeting, but the president had the feeling that his mode of dress would have been no different even if he had known. He seemed to be a man of little pretense.

"Adam." Ted Larkspur stepped forward to perform the necessary introductions.

"Ted." Adam Tchartoff acknowledged Larkspur with a nod, his eyes questioningly on the man behind him.

"Mr. President, Mr. Tchartoff. He understands that our meeting is completely secret."

"Mr. Tchartoff," the president said.

Adam Tchartoff accepted the president's outstretched hand. He was cordial, but he displayed no emotion beyond a polite interest. Nor did he visibly respond when the single Secret Serviceman was dismissed with a wave of the hand after drinks had been served, and he and Ted and the president had been left alone at a white wrought-iron table that overlooked the pleasant expanse of lawn.

"I have a proposition for you," the president said.

"So I'd assumed," Adam Tchartoff replied. "I was asked by your own government to travel as Michael Adams. That makes your need of me rather obvious, doesn't it?" His gaze hadn't wavered from the president's once, and he sat very still, his hands resting on the chair arms, his legs casually crossed. He grinned, and the severity of his features was somewhat lessened.

By God, he's really quite young, the president thought. He was, in fact, at an age when laughter should have come easily.

"Yes, obvious. How's your Scotch?" the president asked.

"Fine, thanks." He shrugged, then lit a cigarette from a pack in his pocket. "I don't mean to be presumptuous, sir, but you did go through a lot of trouble and expense to bring me here. I think we should get down to business. Why?"

The president looked to Ted, who remained silent. He found himself growing restive beneath Tchartoff's unwavering gaze. He stood, moving the ice around in his glass.

"Smoking is bad for your health," he commented.

"So are grenades." Tchartoff laughed. He lifted his glass and shrugged pleasantly again. "I live with the one, might as well live with the other, too."

"You've heard about the recent kidnappings of certain American military men, diplomats, even businessmen, I presume?" the president asked.

Tchartoff's eyes narrowed slightly. "The most recent wave of terrorism against the United States? Everyone has heard—the media definitely give these guys all the exposure they could want. Hijackings, explosions, kidnappings. Bombing raids. Yes, I know what's going on. And we both know my current partners are behind it, don't we?" He drew on his cigarette, his eyes never leaving the president's.

"They're holding some very important men," Ted Larkspur said quietly.

Adam Tchartoff shrugged. "I understand that a secret source revealed that the kidnappers would attempt to negotiate soon. I happen to know that they're not quite ready. That they plan to strike again."

"Yes, that's what we'd heard," the president said.

Tchartoff lifted one brow.

"I want to fight back," the president said.

Adam Tchartoff smiled slowly, leaning back slightly and exhaling smoke. His eyes flickered to the lawn, then back to the president. "That's where I come in, I take it? You don't want to indulge in any bombing, and total warfare is, of course, out. But you'll have to do something, won't you? You can't let your hostages be sacrificed, but then again, you don't really want to be caught negotiating, either, do you? It's a dilemma."

The president wasn't sure whether he was being mocked or not. "I'm sorry for you, Tchartoff," he said at last, "if you've forgotten that every life is sacred."

The blue gaze didn't waver. "I haven't forgotten, sir. Now, why am I here?"

"Eight men are being held. Bright, able men. Four military advisers, two diplomats and two bankers. What the hell anyone would want with a banker..." He shook his head. "Every one of those men has a family. Tearful wives, kids, parents, sisters and brothers—calling. We promise them that we're doing everything we can." He grinned dryly, but no humor touched his aging eyes. "People are calling the radio stations and saying that the United States ought to step in and bomb the entire Mideast—clean out the cesspool! Then again, we're being inundated with calls from people who think I'm a warmonger and should be shot. I don't want a war. I don't want children killed. I don't want a bunch of innocent bystanders killed. I want to infiltrate the group that's responsible, and I want every last one of their hides."

"Tall order," Tchartoff commented. He leaned forward and crushed out his cigarette. Then he leaned back again, his gaze uncompromising.

So suddenly that Tchartoff's muscles contracted, the president slammed a fist against the table. "I will not be terrorized by those bloody murdering bastards!"

Tchartoff raised one brow slightly but said nothing. He glanced over to Ted Larkspur, who seemed determined to keep silent.

"Mr. Tchartoff, we know where the men are being held—and by whom."

"That's to your advantage," Tchartoff said simply.

"They're on an island in the Caribbean," the president continued. "The Death Squad has an entire complex of buildings and bunkers there."

"I assume," Tchartoff said, sipping his Scotch, "you're not intending to blow up the island."

"We can't blow up the island—and you damn well know it. I'd kill my own people. And if this operation isn't carried off perfectly, it will be seen as more aggression on our part."

"I see." Tchartoff lit another cigarette. "You know who they are and where they are. What do you intend to do about it?"

"We don't have time to get a man on the inside. But you're already there—and we want your help."

Tchartoff remained silent for a moment; then he laughed. "You want me to sacrifice the progress I have made to date and rescue your men? One man—against how many?"

"Twelve on this island, we're almost certain."

"You have a lot of faith, sir."

"Yes, I do. I've studied you."

"Exactly what do you want?"

"Well, that's rather obvious, isn't it? I want you to release the American men—and then I want you to blow the compound sky-high."

Tchartoff whistled softly, then laughed. "Why should I risk my life?" he asked. "Hell—it's almost

certain suicide. I'm not an American—I'm an Israeli."

"Yes, I know. And if you're caught and your real
identity discovered, they, too, will know that you're an
Israeli."

Tchartoff slowly started to laugh again. "I see. If I
bungle the whole thing, the United States will have had
no involvement."

"Yes, that's it."

"If I cause those poor patsies to get bullet holes
through their heads, you'll be able to commiserate
with the families."

"That's right. But you'll have all the help the
American military can provide at your disposal."

Tchartoff shook his head. "This is crazy. You
haven't answered me yet. Why should I become involved?"

"You were an American once. The United States
gave you and your family a home when you had none
elsewhere."

"I settled that debt, sir. I paid it off with three years
of tramping through godforsaken rice fields."

"The United States taught you how to fight."

"And how to kill. I grant you that. I even learned
how not to be afraid for my own damn skin."

"I don't think the United States did that, son."

Larkspur watched the president, who was still
holding his trump card. He had to play it carefully.

The president leaned toward Tchartoff. "The men
holding them are your...allies, members of the Death
Squad."

"We've already established that."

"They've not only blown up half of Israel, but your wife and child, as well."

The pulse was beating in the hollow of Tchartoff's throat, and his face had taken on an ashen pallor.

The president leaned back. "Mr. Tchartoff, we have proof of that, and I'll gladly see that you're supplied with it. I grant you, I'm after revenge. I want it so badly it's like choking, night and day. I think you want it, too. And I think I'm supplying you with the one and only real chance you'll have."

"You have proof?"

"I do."

"I want to see what you've got."

"Of course."

Tchartoff rose casually, stuck his hands in his pockets and ambled toward the lawn. He turned to the president with a shrug. "Want to tell me what you've got in mind?"

Chapter 3

Adam shoved his hands into his pockets as he moved along the street, smiling slightly at the garish beauty of the bright neon lights. It was late, but the usual hawkers were still out. Prostitutes were selling their wares not ten feet from the theatergoers, resplendent with their minks and sables and silver hair.

New York, New York. There was nothing like it.

Some said that a big city was a big city, but Adam didn't think so. Oh, they were alike in some ways. London, New York, Paris—even Tokyo. They all had their blend of humanity. A multitude of languages, a multitude of faces, blending together, scurrying around. But each had its own tone, its own throbbing pace that made it unique.

One of the prostitutes called out to him with a welcoming smile. He turned, and when she looked into his eyes, her smile slowly faded, and she hurried down the street.

He pulled up his collar. It was almost summer, but the nights still carried a chill. Breath mingled with exhaust fumes and the steam from the sewers to create a low-lying blanket of mist.

He passed a church, almost tripping over one of the bums who lay sprawled over the steps.

"Got a quarter?" the man whined.

Adam laughed dryly. "Whatever happened to a dime?"

"Inflation, man. Inflation."

Adam dug in his pocket for a dollar. What the hell, he had a wide-open expense account for once in his life.

"Thanks!" the bum called out delightedly.

"My pleasure," Adam said dryly.

He turned down the avenue. Things were quieter here; the streets more deserted—more respectable. Most of the store windows were covered with bars.

His footsteps slowed without conscious thought; he discovered that he was peering between steel bars to stare at a full-length mink in a gray so soft and radiant it was like spun silver.

Sonia would love such a coat, he thought, then gave himself an angry shake. Sonia would have loved such a coat. He had to stop thinking of her in the present tense.

Yet a smile tugged at the corner of his lips as he stared at the coat. Perhaps it was not so bad. He could think of her and smile at the memories. Sonia, who could don khaki, bind up her hair and run blithely to the front of a battle line, could also gasp with delight over a fur, swirl like a princess in silk and purr like a kitten in bed.

Had. She *had* done all those things.

Funny how he couldn't get it right in his mind. Maybe because he'd never really seen her. He'd seen men die in almost every conceivable fashion: shot, knifed, burned, exploded. He'd killed men in almost every conceivable fashion himself—that happened when survival became the issue.

But when they'd brought him to see the charred bodies of his wife and child, he just hadn't been able to see *them*. His mind had just rebelled. It hadn't been Sonia, and it hadn't been Reba.

If Sonia had died on the line, died fighting, he might have managed to handle it. Because still, after all these years, he had the sense that there was a right and a wrong. There were battlefields, and then there were places where people lived. Where they shopped, where they mailed their letters. Where they went for long walks and played in parks.

Children, babies, infants . . . just had no place in it.

A cold sweat coated his body, and he gave himself a little shake, then started down the street again, glancing at his wristwatch. He was late.

But the memories had come on strong. So strong that he paused before a model dressed in a T-shirt and jeans. The dummy was posed with hands on hips, body slightly tilted, a beautiful, mischievous smile in place.

So much like Sonia. Even the hair—dark, flyaway. She had been in jeans the day he'd met her. She'd been trying to change the tire on an old Volkswagen. He'd offered to help, but she'd refused him, cheerfully saying that she had things under control. Then the rim and the tire had flown off in her hands; she'd landed on her rear in the mud—and laughed at herself.

"Well, of course I can do it myself. But I suppose, if you're willing, I can also use some help!"

She'd never been in a man's bed before, but she was in his that night. For her, it had not been a question of morality; it had been a question of what she wanted. And she wanted him. He could remember the feel of her that night. Like satin. She'd been young and firm and incredibly beautiful, and touching the fullness of her breast had been intoxicating. He'd never known such an intense feeling of satisfaction as he had from her, yet it was the aftermath that stayed with him, that haunted him.

She'd asked him how he'd become an American when his mother was an Israeli. He'd explained that he should have been Russian, or Polish, and she'd thought he was kidding. He had laughed, too, then started whispering obscene things to her in Russian. In the end she had laughed some more, and they'd made love again. When they were done that time, she got him talking about the service, about the jungle, about the terror of being in a war. He'd learned then that she was still in the military; she'd talked about it easily.

"It's just something we do here, Adam. It wasn't so long after the war that I was born. We were raised knowing that we must always fight, that we must preserve our land to preserve our lives."

She was fascinated by his command of languages.

"It's a gift," she told him.

"You're a gift," he'd responded. And she'd laughed and told him that she'd known his Russian had been dirty, but she wanted him to say beautiful things to her in Italian and French—weren't those the languages for lovers?

In the days that followed, he began to see Israel through her eyes. Her commander came to meet him one day, and he found himself engaged in a full-scale discussion of munitions and explosives. He'd seen Sonia and the man exchange glances, and that night, with her hair tangled across his bare chest, he'd asked her if she was seducing him for herself or for the Israeli military.

"Both," she had admitted eagerly. "Adam, we need you. You're vibrant, you're a fighter! You're part of all this. It's in your blood, whether you wish to admit it or not. We need you...."

"We?" he'd asked her, and despite her gentle touch, his body had stiffened.

"I need you...."

And it was true. She needed him. Israel needed him. The United States was allegedly at peace.

He married Sonia; he became an Israeli. He took a special-assignments job with the government, and he kept fighting.

It had taken five years for Reba to come along. And Sonia, despite her desire to keep working, had never been so ecstatic over anything as she had been over motherhood. They'd lain one night with the baby between them, checking her fingers and toes and laughing over her fuzzy black hair. And Sonia had said, "Oh, Lord, Adam! That we have created her... I love her so much it terrifies me." She'd shuddered then, almost as if she'd had a premonition. "Oh, Adam! We must promise ourselves—if something should happen to me, you must love her all your life. You must guard her all your life...."

He'd laughed. Sonia's job was at a desk then. "Nothing is going to happen to you. We will grow old and fat together and make her insane because we won't let her date until she's thirty."

Sonia hadn't laughed. "Promise me, Adam!" He had seen how serious she was, so he had kissed her tenderly and held her, and sworn that he would joyfully protect both of them with his life....

But he'd never had a chance to exchange his life for theirs.

A passerby walked a wide berth around Adam, and he realized that he was staring at a dummy in a T-shirt, and that his hands were clenched into tight fists at his sides. He started walking again. Now he was really late for his appointment.

He quickened his pace, and moments later hurried down the steps to Astors. Toni was already there, alone as he had requested. He was supposed to be a tourist, and tourists always saw their relatives. They partied, they had a good time.

And in this case, Uncle Sam would pick up the check.

"Adam!"

His cousin, radiantly smiling, threw herself into his arms before he reached the table. He returned the embrace, then set her from him. She was too slim, he thought, but that was the way Toni liked to be. She was healthy, anyway. Her cheeks were nice and scrubbed pink, and her dark eyes were brilliant. Her hair was chopped short, blow-styled, chic. Very New York, Adam thought with a grin tugging at his lip.

She's already ordered his Scotch, neat. It was on the table.

"Adam!" she said again, sitting across from him. He knew that she was studying him. She didn't say that he looked good; she gave him the same curious gaze the prostitute on the street had given him. Except that her smile didn't fade.

"How are you?" she asked anxiously.

"Good," he told her, taking a sip of his Scotch, then idly running a finger down the glass. He gave her a smile. "And you. I saw the play—you were great."

"Oh, Adam! It was off-, off-, way off-Broadway. But you came, you really came? You saw it all?"

"Heard every word!"

"Thanks," she said softly. Then, "What are you doing here?"

He shrugged and pulled out a cigarette and lit it slowly, casually. "Just visiting," he said at last.

"You should have warned me! I would have planned more than a late-night drink. How long are you staying?"

"I leave tomorrow morning—caught one of those cheap charter rates to Paris. I thought I'd tour around a bit. Maybe catch a few of the Greek Islands." He didn't want Toni to know that he might be back in the United States. Toni didn't know anything about Michael Adams. With any luck, she never would.

She breathed a little sigh as if she were relieved. "Oh, God, Adam, I'm so glad to see you doing things. That's what you need, you know. Are you really okay?"

He forced a smile into his features. "Sure."

"You're—over it?"

"Oh, come on, Toni! You know people never really get over things like that. Am I stable and functioning? Yes—can't you tell?"

She laughed and stirred her drink. "Yes, I guess so, Adam. I just wish—well, I wish your mom had never left the States. I wish you'd never gone to Israel. God help me, because I loved Sonia, but I wish that you'd never met her."

He lowered his lashes, staring at his glass. She was treading on dangerous ground—ground he never entered himself.

"Don't say that, Toni," he warned.

She might have blushed; he couldn't really tell. "Of course, I'm sorry. You really were such beautiful people, she so dark and lovely, you so gloriously blond and tanned and muscled! But don't you see, Adam? I think that's half your problem. You're trying to replace Sonia—"

"Toni!" he admonished in exasperation, looking at her, and even she quailed a little at his glance.

She tossed back her head and picked up her drink a little belligerently. "Sorry, Adam. What are you going to do—shoot me?"

"Toni—"

"Oh, Adam! I really am horribly sorry!" There was true regret in her tone; Adam edged his teeth together. Maybe the subject could be changed now. "Forgive me?" she said softly.

"Toni, of course—"

"I'm just going to say one more thing, Adam, and then I'll promise to keep my mouth shut. You're looking for a goddamned heroine, and they just don't come in packages, you know!"

"Toni, leave it." He paused, his mouth tightening, his thoughts suddenly shifting. As Toni spoke, he conjured up another face. A very different face. Seagreen eyes, a wild mass of tawny blond curls.

It was the woman he had seen from the park bench and then again at the memorial, with Ted Larkspur. There had been something about her.... She had met his eyes, for one thing. She hadn't looked away, and she had never denied to herself that she was staring at him. There had been something courageous in that gaze; it had caught his attention when nothing else could.

He remembered how she had been dressed at the memorial. He could remember everything about her, he realized. She had been dressed simply, with an attractive, understated sophistication. The lady came from money. Washington society. She wasn't the type of woman he needed now. Right now it didn't matter who a woman was; it barely mattered what she looked like, as long as she was clean. He had realized that so long as he still breathed, he had basic needs. But he felt like an emotional void; he had nothing to give in return.

Still, she had interested him. He had even acknowledged to himself that he found her to be very beautiful, and perhaps more. There seemed to be so much life and emotion and passion within her eyes.

It was probably a good thing he was leaving the country. She meant something to Larkspur, and he liked Larkspur. He shouldn't associate with anyone close to the man.

"Adam? Did you hear me?"

"Yes, yes. You said that I needed a heroine. Damn you, Toni—"

Toni held up her hand. "I'm done! I'm done! Why don't you plan to stay a few more days, Adam? I'd love to have a little get-together—"

"I can't stay, Toni. I've already made my travel arrangements."

"So you change them!"

"I can't," he said flatly. Then he looked at her. "Hey—if you want, you can come out and spend some time with me in between shows."

"Uh-uh," she said emphatically. "I already did the whole Israeli thing, you know. That time I came out before and stayed all those months. First of all my damned luggage was stolen—everything I owned! Then they searched me—and refused to let me get on the plane as they were suspicious—because I'd been there three months and didn't have any luggage! No thanks, Adam. I love you like a brother—or as much as you let anyone love you!—but not again."

"Hey—we haven't had a hijacking in years," he reminded her, a little tersely, she thought. "I'd say we have the safest airlines in the world."

She looked at the table and spoke softly. "I'm an American, Adam. Nothing else. I've no desire to be anything else. I don't want the violence, I don't want the desert, I don't want any of it! Terrorism is taking over, and I want safely out of it, thank you."

He wasn't going to argue with her—their time together was too brief. He turned the conversation back to her play, and they talked about the world at large.

She hugged him goodbye. "Adam—take care. Let things go lightly for a while, huh?"

He grinned engagingly, or what would have been engagingly, if only the warmth had touched his eyes. They seemed to glitter in the muted hallway light. "Sure. Hey, I'm on vacation, aren't I?"

He tweaked her chin as he had often done when they were kids; he the older cousin, she the adoring little girl in tow.

Adam walked away, giving her a last cheery wave. An arresting man in a smart leather jacket and jeans, blond hair catching the soft light.

Except that it was an illusion. There was nothing soft about him.

Cannes
May 22

It hadn't been difficult to arrange Michael Adams's meeting with the leader of Cell Six of the Death Squad—or Freedom International, as the group chose to identify itself when members happened to meet with the press. They were to have lunch at the Café Antoine near the beach, a rather stereotypical French sidewalk café with red and white striped sun umbrellas set atop the tables. Men and women sipped their coffees or espressos or mineral waters and dined on cheese, watching the passersby or looking at the beach, where the beautiful and the not-so-beautiful stretched their naked and near-naked bodies beneath the sun.

Adam saw Ali Abdul as soon as he entered the café. There were other Arabs at some of the tables, but there was something striking about the man Adam had come to see. He was in his sixties, wearing a burnoose, and he barely moved as his sunken eyes surveyed the street before him. He was not alone. He was with a younger man in a business suit, a dark, intense man of about forty.

That was Khazar Abdul, Adam knew, Ali's son, and next in line for cell leadership. Whereas Ali was rumored to be cool, collected and rational at all times, Khazar was known to be a hothead. Ali murdered for a reason—Khazar lived with a hatred that made him volatile, at best.

Adam paused briefly, his eyes scanning the rest of the patrons. He was certain the Abduls were far from alone. The café was filled with tourists of many nationalities: French, Italian, Arab, Spanish, German, Swiss, English and American. But they weren't all tourists. Abdul would not risk the chance of assassination.

Adam moved forward, heading for Ali's table. A man stood and brushed against him. He felt the gun in Adam's jacket pocket and reached deftly beneath the material for it. In accented French he apologized for his clumsiness. Adam lifted his hands and assured him, "*De rien.* It's nothing." They weren't going to let him get close to Ali with a weapon.

He went over to the table, feeling tension constrict his throat. These men had been responsible for the death of his wife and child. His muscles were tightening. He had to relax. He had to forget. For now.

Ali Abdul was on his feet, greeting Adam like an old friend, giving him a kiss on each cheek. Khazar rose more stiffly than his father, but he, too, went through the motions of a friendly greeting, his dark eyes studying Adam intently.

He doesn't trust me, Adam thought. But then, he was certain that Khazar didn't trust anyone.

"So you are Michael Adams," Ali said quietly when they were all seated. The old man's eyes were sunken. His health could not be good.

"Yes, I am Michael Adams."

"And you are anxious to join our little group in our endeavors."

"I am."

"Why?" Khazar asked.

His father cast him a warning glare. To Adam, Ali offered a rueful grin. "Yes, we are curious as to why. Many of our number fight for religion—"

"And many do not," Adam said.

"And many fight for our support in their struggles against the oppressors in their homelands."

Half the revolutionaries in South America wanted an in, Adam knew.

He leaned back in his chair, summoned the waiter and asked for an espresso. He waited until the demitasse was set down and the waiter was gone before he answered. "The money, gentlemen. I'm sure that my reputation preceded me, just as I came to you because of all I had heard. I may bear a few grudges against a certain superpower, but my concern isn't religion or freedom. In fact, it isn't really anything at all except that I want the money, and..." He paused, leaning forward. "I like the action."

He had Khazar now. The man knew what it was like to savor power. Khazar liked to kill, too, Adam thought.

For Ali, perhaps this was a holy war. But not for his son.

A chill snaked along Adam's spine. He didn't like Khazar. The man was someone to watch, to avoid. If Ali should happen to die in the midst of this, then God help them all.

"What do you have to offer?" Ali asked.

Adam smiled, folding his hands in his lap. "Contacts, gentlemen. The U.S. government doesn't know what to think of me. They want me on their side. They're ready to woo me. I can go places the very best of you can't reach."

"But how do we know you're really on our side, then?" Khazar asked sharply.

"You'll have to test me, won't you?" Adam asked.

"Yes," Ali murmured, watching him carefully. "We shall have to test you. And I have the perfect situation in mind." He rested his arms on the table and leaned close to Adam. He began to speak slowly, describing what he wanted, watching Adam all the while. His eyes were old, but very sharp. As Adam listened, he felt tension coiling in his stomach again. The rumors had been right. And now he knew where the next action was going to take place, and who was going to be their next target.

"You will make sure the senator is where he is supposed to be," Ali told him.

"And then . . ." Khazar said, his eyes dark, intense, deadly. "Then you will come to the compound. When the mission is complete, we will know that you are one of us. And if you are not..." He paused for effect, Adam knew. His cup was in his hand, thick pottery.

The cup cracked and broke. Khazar smiled.

"If not, I will see to your death myself. And you may trust in the fact that I am a master, an artist, at death."

Adam smiled. He felt very cold. Khazar could not know that he was a master at death himself. This was between them, he thought. He knew, sitting there, meeting the two men, that Khazar had caused the death of his family. To Ali, those murders would have been pointless. To Khazar, they would have been pleasure.

Adam sipped his espresso, then lifted his cup to Khazar. "I will prove myself to you, Monsieur Abdul." He looked at Ali. "When shall I leave?"

"Tonight. You must go home tonight. I want to have the senator in my hands with the others by the first of July. On the fourth I will have my men returned to me, or I will kill an American for the celebration of his independence."

Chapter 4

The Templeton house was ablaze with lights. Chinese lanterns were strewn all around the gardens and the lawns. The pool reflected the colored shades with a mesmerizing beauty. The people in attendance were decked out in splendor, too, the men in tuxedos, the women in silks and satins and velvets, some demure, some startling, all created by the most famous designers. It was a Washington society party, and society was there in force. The president wasn't in attendance, so the place wasn't crawling with security, but there were a number of congressmen present, so Amber knew that some of the men moving around the room were probably security.

She hadn't really wanted to come to this party, but her father had asked her, and despite her wealth and popularity and importance, Helen Templeton was one of the nicest women Amber had ever met. It was just that she was anxious to leave—she and Josie and Myra were due to start their vacation late the next day, and she still hadn't packed.

The waiting hadn't been half as hard as she had expected. She had even been somewhat disturbed at herself, because she wasn't as miserable as she had expected to be. She had spent time with her father. She had gone to lunch with friends. And she hadn't really thought about Peter, not at all. In fact, when she *had* dreamed, she had been haunted by the man with the ice-blue eyes, the man who had disappeared after the memorial service. She would most probably never see him again, she thought. And yet he walked through her dreams. He strode through them, and though they didn't speak or touch, his eyes were on her, and she could not look away from them. One morning she realized that she had awakened to wonder what it would be like to go to bed with such a man, and then she really *was* disturbed. Her life, as she had lived it for so long, had fallen apart—and she wasn't mourning a deep, long-term relationship, she was wondering about a stranger who had walked away into the sunset of life. And even as she danced on the terrace with her father, watching the play of the lights over the water, she was thinking of that man.

"There's Senator Daldrin," her father muttered suddenly. "I need to speak with him. Do you mind?"

Amber pulled away from him. "Of course not, Dad. You know that I'm a big girl. I'll be all right on my own."

He smiled and excused himself. Amber wandered over to the buffet table and reached for a glass, planning to pour herself some punch.

A hand closed over the glass, a masculine hand, long bronze fingers brushing over hers and bringing an instant flood of sensation washing through her. She looked up quickly.

It was him. The man from the memorial service. The man from the park. The man with the striking light-blue eyes and rugged features. He hadn't disappeared into the sunset. He was standing behind Helen Templeton's buffet table, and he was going to pour her a glass of punch.

His eyes were meeting hers just as they had in her dreams, and the intensity of his eyes and the brush of his fingers against hers were doing more to her than she had ever imagined any man could.

"May I?" he asked politely. She liked his voice. She liked the depth of it, the timbre, the way it seemed to swirl around her. He was wearing a tuxedo with a starched white pleated shirt and vest, and he couldn't have been more elegantly dressed. He wore the tux well. She might have thought that the very ruggedness of his appeal would make him stiff or uncomfortable in formal wear, but in fact the outfit enhanced his masculinity and made him all the more striking.

"Thank you," she said, releasing the glass. He poured out a measure of punch, and when she took it from him she felt the brush of his fingers again. Once more their glances met, and she was fascinated by the fire that seemed to burn within his eyes, despite their ice-blue shade.

She sipped her punch, thinking that perhaps he would ask her to dance. Then she wondered why he had bothered to pour her punch, because he suddenly looked as if he disliked her. His gaze swept over her, and she thought that he was going to turn away. To stop him, she found herself speaking quickly, her hand extended to him. "I'm Amber Larkspur. Ted's daughter. You know my father. I saw you speaking with him."

His brow arched, and he hesitated. Then his hand took hers. "I know. I've seen you with your father."

A small smile curved her lips. She'd met secretive types before—Washington sometimes seemed filled with them—but seldom had she seen the attitude taken quite so far.

"Pardon me. I don't mean to be rude, but do you have a name?"

He smiled then, and she liked the smile. It was rueful and honest, and maybe hadn't been intended. "Michael Adams, Miss Larkspur," he said very softly. And then, "Do you dance?"

"Well, certainly, Mr. Adams, I do."

He kept her hand and led her to the dance floor on the terrace. The music had been fast; now it was slow, and he pulled her into his arms to the softly pulsing strains of a popular ballad. Her fingers fell upon the coarse fabric of his jacket, and she found herself inhaling the scent of the man, a clean scent, lightly touched with after-shave. His hand rested on the small of her back and held her close, but not too close; she wasn't uncomfortable at all. The fingers of his other hand curled around hers, and he led her across the floor, moving with a surprising grace. Just as his appearance in the tux had surprised her, so did the fact that he knew how to dance so well. How to hold a woman close, how to touch her.

Her head fell back slightly, and she looked into his eyes. She was startled by the intensity of his gaze, then felt as if the fire of it was flooding through her. A rose tint colored her cheeks as she realized that she was thinking about going to bed with this man again. She didn't know him at all, but when she looked at him, when she felt his touch, she wanted to forget the past and the future and imagine that the present could go on forever. He wasn't holding her too closely, and yet she knew that his thoughts were running dangerously parallel to her own. She knew from his eyes that though he might want to keep his distance from her, he was fascinated in spite of himself. He might not have wanted to give her even so much as his name, but strip away their environs, their hostess and the guests, the fabrics, the silks and the satins, the Chinese lanterns . . . strip it all down to the basics, and he wanted her, too.

She swallowed convulsively, thinking that they'd barely exchanged a few dozen words, and yet intimate, forbidden things were taking place between them. She wanted to pull away, to run from him as she had never run in her life. But stronger than the urge to run was the desire to know. To go on touching him. To find out where this might lead...

She needed to speak, to do something to break the tension between them. She moistened her lips and smiled, and yet she felt that there could be no small talk between them, that whatever she said had to be honest.

"I saw you in the park," she said.

"Yes," he told her.

"Are you with the government?"

He hesitated for a second. "Perhaps. I'm not sure yet. I'm thinking of taking a job."

Security, Amber thought. It had to be a security position.

"I've been out of the country for a long time," he supplied.

"Business or pleasure?"

He was quiet for a moment, his hand moving against the small of her back. He seemed to look down at her from a great height, and a shield of ice seemed to have fallen over his eyes. "You *are* forward, Miss Larkspur."

"Am I?" And he didn't answer questions very well. But he'd been watching Ian Daldrin. He had to be considering a security position with the senator.

"Um. Business and pleasure," he said. "And all over."

"All over?"

"I've been all over the globe, Miss—"

"Amber. Please." She felt as if he knew her inside and out, and he was still calling her Miss Larkspur.

He smiled suddenly. " 'Forever Amber'?" he queried softly. His words, his whisper, just touched her ear. "I saw the movie. Does your nature run so freely and passionately, too?"

"Now *you're* being forward."

"Yes, but I gave you an answer."

This was the time to end it, to pull away and never see him again. She would let him remain in her heart, a fantasy. But she didn't pull away. Instead she moved with him, moved on the air. She felt the dip and sway of the Chinese lanterns, felt his eyes, felt the magic of the colored lights rippling on the water. And she kept her gaze level with his.

She felt as if his hand was trembling slightly, as if he wanted to pull her closer. As if the frost had left his eyes for a brief moment. Then he did pull her close, and for a moment they touched so fully that she felt his startling heat and vibrance from her breast down to her thighs. Then he released her, and she realized the music had stopped.

"Amber!" She heard her father's voice. He was standing behind her, his tone sharp.

Michael Adams stepped away, but his eyes remained on her. "Mr. Larkspur," he said, acknowledging her father's presence but still watching Amber. "Thank you for the dance, Miss Larkspur," he said.

Then he turned and disappeared into the crowd. The music started again, and her father pulled her into his arms, but she was still staring after Michael.

"Amber!"

"What?" She looked into her father's eyes. They were troubled and severe.

"Stay—" He paused, swallowing. He hadn't told her what she could and couldn't do in years. "Stay away from—from Adams."

"Why? Who is he?"

"You—"

"Security?"

"We . . . we haven't decided yet. Amber, he's dangerous."

"It sounds as if you don't like him."

"No, I do like him. I like him very much. I just want you to stay away from him."

"Why?"

"Why?" Her father was silent for a long moment. "He was in Vietnam—"

"Dad! Half the men I know were in Vietnam!"

"Damn it, Amber, just listen to me for once. Stay away from Michael Adams. For my peace of mind." Angry, he released her, and Amber found herself alone on the dance floor, staring after the second man to leave her there.

It wasn't long before she was claimed again. Timothy Hawkins, the youngest rep from the great state of Kansas, slipped up behind her and offered her a broad grin. "Amber! You're back in Washington! Is it too much to hope that you might be alone?"

"Very much alone, Tim," she replied, accepting his arm. He whirled her around happily. He was tall, with friendly hazel eyes and a freckled face, and she liked

him very much. But even as she smiled and laughed
and responded to his questions, she wondered how it
could feel so different to dance with him. No quickening breath, no slow fire touching her soul.

So Michael Adams was dangerous, in her father's
estimation. But her father liked him; he had admitted
that, He liked him—but he still thought he was dangerous.

She wondered whether she could make that matter
or not.

He couldn't stay there. He couldn't talk to Daldrin
or Larkspur or any of the others. He had to leave the
terrace.

With a stiff Scotch in his hand, he hurried down one
of the garden paths and came to a trellised arbor with
a black wrought-iron bench. Sitting, he found himself loosening his tie. He was hot, burning up from
dancing.

No, it wasn't from dancing. It was the woman.

What was it about her? She was attractive, yes. She
had beautiful flowing light hair that smelled wonderful. Her shoulders were bare beneath the slim strips of
the kelly-green silk she was wearing. Her skin was
ivory, she was slim, with beautiful hollows and curves,
and she had fit into his arms as he had rarely felt any
woman do. There was warmth to her, there was
laughter, and there was that flare of passion and determination and bravado within her eyes. Eyes the
color of the Caribbean. Green and blue and beguil-
ing. From the moment he had seen her across the

room, he had known that he should stay away from
her. She was Ted Larkspur's daughter, and he liked
Ted Larkspur. And he wasn't going to fall in love; love
was dead within him. But from the moment he had
seen her tonight, he had known that he wanted her.
Wanted to bed her. Wanted to be with her. He didn't
want to know about tomorrow; he just wanted to have
her, to feel her move beneath him. He had watched her
on the dance floor, watched the length of leg displayed when her skirt swirled around her. Watched the
laughter and the love when she looked into her father's eyes. But when she had looked into his eyes, he
had seen more, much more. He had seen passion, seen
electricity that could spark and burn and rise in sweet,
fantastic flames. The room had faded, and he had
known that he needed to leave. Now fury touched his
soul. He couldn't have her, and that was that, and it
was ridiculous to want to touch a woman so badly, any
woman. The woman he had loved was gone, and others did not matter. One had to be the same as any
other.

But she wasn't. His wanting wasn't logical, and it
couldn't be reasoned away, and no matter how furious he grew with her, it wasn't her fault that she was
beautiful and charismatic and had a smile that caused
a quivering deep within him.

He swallowed a long gulp of Scotch, winced as it
burned its way down to his gullet and turned to the
house. From the shadow of the arbor he could see her
again. She was with a younger man. He narrowed his
eyes, quickly placing everyone he had met that night.

Timothy Hawkins, the congressman from Kansas. A nice kid, if just a bit wet behind the ears. Still full of integrity and idealism. One day, maybe, he could be a force to be reckoned with—if he had the power and the charm.

She made a perfect match for Hawkins. She possessed the same charm, and she was laughing in his arms. Adam couldn't see the color of her eyes, and yet he felt that he could see their sparkle and sizzle. He could feel the sweep of her silken hair over his fingers, brushing his chin.

"Damn it!" he swore aloud, then chuckled. Toni would enjoy this. Maybe she would think he was alive at last.

"When I need it the least!" he muttered, but he stretched his legs out and leaned back, and he kept watching Amber dance.

Maybe it wasn't wrong to watch her, to want her.

No. To want any woman so intensely couldn't be right.

The punch was potent. Very potent. The dancing had made her hot, and the alcohol level in the punch hadn't helped a bit.

Determined to have a good time, Amber had danced and laughed and talked, then danced some more. Ian Daldrin had seemed depressed, so she had tried to spend time with him, talking, drawing him out. Josie and Myra had come, and they had talked about their plans and agreed to meet at the airport. Then she had danced with Timothy again. And then, hot and flushed, she had glimpsed the little arbor with its profusion of roses and started toward it for a few moments alone. The night had been difficult for her. She had learned long ago, for her father's sake, to smile through almost anything. But her smile, she thought, was fading fast.

Sipping her punch, she ducked beneath the spray of roses, then started, standing still as she realized that she was not alone. The light was behind her, and for a moment she didn't know who she was facing. Then she realized that it was Michael Adams. She could tell by his scent, by the way he was standing, by the electricity that seemed to charge the small arbor. He had been sitting, but he stood quickly when she arrived, and now he was staring at her.

"I'm sorry," she said awkwardly. "I didn't mean to intrude."

"You're not intruding," he said quickly. It was a lie. But he didn't say more, nor did he move. He just stood there.

As her eyes became more accustomed to the light, she could see his face, could see the way he was looking at her. "I think I am intruding," she said very softly. "I think you wish I would disappear into the air. Isn't that true?"

He was silent for a long moment before speaking. "Yes," he said then.

She had started to turn away, but he caught her arm and swung her around. She came up flush with his body. His arm held her, and his eyes seared into her.

"And no," he added softly.

She felt the warmth and the crush of his body, and the response she had forbidden herself came to life within her, fast fire lapping through her. She stared at his mouth and thought that it was a hard mouth, yet she wanted to know what it would feel like if he kissed her.

"Yes," he said again very softly. "And...no."

Then his lips touched hers. There was nothing soft about his kiss, nothing gentle. It was everything that she had imagined it might be: volatile and passionate and demanding, even shocking. His mouth closed over hers, his tongue demanding entrance, then stroking the inside of her mouth with an intimacy that suggested much more. She placed her hands against his chest, meaning to protest, but then there was no protest. He kissed her hard, and he kissed her long, probing, discovering with his tongue, touching her ever deeper, until she felt that her body had become a wall of flame. His fingers moved into her hair, tilting her head to meet his demand, then his hand moved over her body, pulling her closer. His fingers closed over her breast, and despite the silk of her gown and the lace of her bra, she felt the caress with such clarity that she was afraid she would fall. A whimper escaped her as his lips traveled to her throat, to the lobe of her ear, to her forehead, then back to her throat. She found herself held tightly in his arms as he sat, bringing her down with him. When she opened her eyes, she was sitting across his lap, his ragged breath touching her cheeks, his eyes on her with wary anger.

Embarrassed suddenly for all that she had allowed him to do, she tried to pull away, but he held her tight. Beneath the fabric of the tuxedo he was made of steel. She couldn't begin to budge his arms. He held her tightly, and he did not smile; he just stared into her eyes. "You need to go home, Miss Larkspur."

"Then let me up," she said. Her lips were damp and swollen, and she was still shaking. He was the angry one; he was the one acting as if something was wrong. And yet his arms were still around her.

He swore suddenly. "Don't you understand? No, I guess you don't." He laughed, a dry, bitter sound. She thought that he would let her up then, but he didn't. Instead he kissed her again. But this time he was gentle. His lips covered hers and moved with a tender and persuasive touch. His knuckles brushed her chin and grazed over her breast, and there was longing in the touch. Something that made her ache to know more. That made her long to shed her clothing there in the grass and give herself to him.

But his lips left hers, and he released her, setting her carefully on the bench. "My God, but I could want you…" he whispered softly. Then he kissed her hand. "Goodbye, Amber Larkspur."

He turned and left the arbor. She gasped for breath, drawing shaky fingers to her lips, and tried to stand, but she couldn't.

She struggled for composure, smoothing her hair and wondering about him. She tried to stop wanting him, telling herself that it was despicable to want a man that way, a man she barely knew, could never know. A dangerous man, or so her father had told her. It was ridiculous. She was supposed to be slowly mending a broken heart; she was supposed to be hurting for Peter, for the life she had left behind.

And she would, she promised herself. She would mourn Peter once again. Just as soon as she could get home and shower and not have to breathe in the haunting scent of Michael Adams, the scent that lingered on her flesh, her gown.

She was Ted Larkspur's daughter, she reminded herself. She stood, squared her shoulders and brought a smile to her trembling lips. Tim had asked her to go sailing as soon as she came back. She was going to do it. And until then, she would be damned if she was going to let memories of the mysterious Mr. Adams mar her thoughts or her future.

Twenty minutes later Adam waited on the front lawn. Senator Daldrin appeared first, then Ted Larkspur, then Jim Reeves, the intelligence liaison. Each man held a drink, and they stood in the center of a pool of light, far from the house, far from the surrounding foliage. They smiled and sipped their drinks as they stood.

"Adam spoke with Ali Abdul. He's being tested with your kidnapping, Ian."

Ian Daldrin didn't blink an eye. He smiled and lifted his Scotch to Adam. "Well, then," he said very softly, "am I to be taken to the island?"

"Yes. I don't know exactly when, though. And it's my responsibility to see that you're available to be easily whisked away."

Daldrin nodded.

"We're gambling, Senator. You know that," Ted advised Ian.

"If I'm on Abdul's list, my life is already a gamble," Ian said, offering Adam a dry smile. "Son, if this is going to happen, I'm glad you're on our team."

"Thank you, Senator. I hope I'm worthy of your confidence."

"You'll be with me?" Ian asked him.

"All the way, sir."

"Then that's that. Jim, any advice?"

"Yes, lie low. Don't fight. Don't protest. Roll with the punches—"

"Now, Jim, I may not be as young as I used to be, but I'd hate to think that I couldn't hold my own—"

"There will be plenty of time for that, sir, I hope," Adam said. "I have the feeling that getting you and me in is going to be fairly easy. Getting everyone out is the trick, and I may need to depend on you then."

"Yes, that's true, isn't it."

"When's it going to happen?"

"On the cruise."

Ian Daldrin frowned. "I have friends sailing with me on that ship."

"I'm sorry, Senator. I don't have any guarantees," Adam said. "But you should be safe enough. Abdul doesn't want trouble. He wants you off, clean and neat. Not a speck of bloodshed. You see, he wants to be far away before the coast guard or the military can be notified. I'll know that night, and I'll see to it that you're able to excuse yourself from the others and get to the proper deck. No one other than you should be hurt or involved in any way.''

Ian Daldrin exhaled slowly and rocked back on his heels. Then he swallowed the tail end of his Scotch. ''Well then, my friends, cheers. God willing, I'll be back with you soon.''

''God willing,'' Larkspur muttered.

Daldrin lifted his empty glass and called out a loud good night. Reeves nodded curtly to Larkspur and Adam, then followed the senator to the house.

Larkspur didn't look at Adam. He stared across the expanse of grass. ''Everything is go, then.''

''Yes.''

Larkspur nodded. ''Take care of yourself, Tchartoff.''

''Thank you. I intend to.''

''Don't communicate with us from the ship. They'll have someone watching you. Don't take any chances, or we could lose everyone.''

''I won't.''

''And don't—''

''Sir,'' Adam interrupted, his voice soft but very firm. ''I know my business.''

''Yes, well, I guess you do. Good luck, then.'' Ted Larkspur started to move away, then paused and turned back. ''Tchartoff?''

''Yes, what is it?''

"Please, stay away from my daughter." Adam stared at him blankly. Ted cleared his throat. "She's just an innocent bystander. I don't want any innocent bystanders hurt."

An ice-cold shield fell over Adam's eyes. "I don't plan on seeing your daughter, Larkspur. I never did." It was his turn to move. He started across the lawn, leaving Ted standing there.

"Wait!" Ted said. Adam looked around carefully, one brow arched as he approached Ted.

"What is it?"

"I just don't want you to get the wrong idea."

"What wrong idea?" Adam offered Ted a dry grin. "I don't blame you for not liking—"

"No, it's not a matter of not liking you. I think you're a first-rate human being, maybe better than you realize yourself. It's just that my daughter is very much alive, Tchartoff. She *is* life, and her very heart is warmth. And you're..."

"Not really alive, and cold as ice," Adam supplied quietly for Larkspur. "Really, sir, I understand. Excuse me, I have a plane to catch tomorrow. I want to get some sleep."

"Wait!" Larkspur insisted one more time.

Adam hesitated. Larkspur gripped his hand and shook it hard. "Come back alive, son. Please God, come back alive."

"Thank you, sir." Adam retrieved his hand, smiled grimly at Larkspur and started across the lawn.

* * *

Sleep was the last thing he was going to get that night.

He lay awake and smoked. He stared at the ceiling in his hotel room, and he kept hearing Ted Larkspur's words. "She *is* life, and her very heart is warmth."

And he was dead. Well, he had felt like death on occasion. Often. Until tonight.

Until he had held her. He'd never meant to kiss her; he'd never meant to touch her. But he had. She was different. She looked different; she behaved differently; she tasted different....

He rolled over with a soft groan, crushing out his cigarette, then turned and stared at the ceiling again. He would like to be on a beach with her. A long, empty stretch of beach. And she'd be dressed almost like she was tonight. She'd be barefoot and wearing some kind of silk dress that he could slip over her shoulders before letting it drift away into the darkness. He'd take time to look at her, he swore it, then he'd take her down onto the sand, and that sexy lion's mane of hair would spill all around them and entangle them both, and her naked flesh would be supple and hot against his....

He sat up, rubbing his temple, lighting another cigarette. When he closed his eyes tightly, the images disappeared, and he brought back a picture of his wife, laughing, and he heard again the echoes of his own laughter.

"I loved you so much!" he whispered aloud. "I loved you so damn much."

Love was dead, and Larkspur was right. He was dead, too.

He threw off the sheet and padded across the room to the dresser, where he poured himself another Scotch. He drank it fast, grateful for the fire that burned in his gullet. In the flicker of moonlight his bare chest and shoulders glistened in the dresser mirror. He was hot. Despite the blast of the air conditioner, he was slick with perspiration.

One more Scotch. He crawled into bed, where the pain curled in on him again, and he winced hard and willed himself to sleep.

Not a mile away, Amber was faring little better. At two o'clock she gave up, rose and turned on the lights, then started packing. At two-thirty she made herself a cup of herbal tea, and when that failed to make her sleepy, she fixed herself a large coffee liqueur with ice.

She packed everything she could think of, then sat on her bed to watch a late movie on cable. But her fingers rose to her lips, and she remembered the taste and feel and excitement of the man who had touched her so intensely, so fiercely....

And so quickly.

She threw her pillow across the room with a vengeance, then glanced at the telephone stand by her bedside. Her heart took a funny little leap. Connie, her father's secretary and housekeeper, had left a message by the phone that she hadn't seen before.

Peter called. Will try again tomorrow, or please try to reach him.

Peter . . .

Peter. Yes, five years of her life, the man she had been engaged to, the man she had wanted to marry.

She exhaled. Peter, yes, Peter . . .

Peter had never, ever kissed her like that.

Never.

Palm Beach, Florida
June 5

By nine o'clock, Amber, Myra and Josie had checked into a room at their hotel. Myra was busy inspecting the courtesy bar and exclaiming over the number of candy bars in it. "My favorite!" she yelped cheerfully. Josie walked out of the bathroom with the complimentary containers of shampoo and conditioner and smiled at Amber. "Aren't these darling?"

"Darling," Amber agreed. She pulled back the curtains and looked at the pool. It was night, but the poolside was busy. "I wonder how late it's open," she mused.

Myra, who had already consumed a candy bar, was looking in the guest services book. "All night," she supplied cheerfully. "Shall we take a swim?"

"Sure," Amber decided.

Within ten minutes they were testing the water. It was just right—cool—and the night was warm, and being in the water was delicious. After a while Myra and Josie opted for the whirlpool, but Amber didn't want anything to do with heat, so she stretched out on a chaise and looked at the sky. By next week, there would be a full moon.

Myra plopped down beside her. "Did you see that guy?"

"What guy?"

"The one with the platinum hair and the bulging biceps."

"Myra, biceps are not everything."

"Well, these were pretty close."

Josie, carefully balancing a trio of piña coladas that looked like yellow-tinged ice-cream shakes, sank down, too. Amber quickly sat up, nabbing a piña colada before it could land on her lap. "You need a tall blonde with biceps," Josie announced.

"Would you shush!" Amber asked them. "I *had* a tall blonde with biceps. If and when I decide I want another one, I'll ask your advice when I go looking, hmm?"

Josie shook her head and turned to Myra. "She's being sarcastic."

"Yes."

"Right. And you two are happily married ladies. So keep your eyes off the guys with the biceps or I'll tell your husbands."

"Idle threats," Josie said.

Myra sighed deeply. "I'm gaining more weight each year. If you don't get married soon, I'm going to look like hell in a bridesmaid's gown."

Amber groaned loudly. "You guys, I said I'd come so we could have a good time together!"

"All right, all right!" Josie agreed. Then she leaped to her feet and pointed toward the lagoon. "Oh, look! They have a fireworks display!"

The three of them were up. They hurried along the path to the lagoon that centered the hotel and its golf course. On the water was a beautiful show of colors and bursting lights.

She was jostled suddenly. A young couple had backed into her by accident. The woman quickly apologized. Amber smiled and told them it was quite all right. Then she watched the pair as they moved away. The man's arm was wrapped protectively around the woman's shoulder. They were enjoying the show, but they were more engrossed with one another than anything else. "Honeymooners, I'll bet," she told herself with a smile. And she thought that if she ever came back, she would want to come with someone she really loved. Someone to share the beauty and the fun, yet who loved and needed her more than any of it.

She found herself thinking not of Peter, but of Michael Adams.

"Amber?" Josie called to her.

"I'm here," Amber called back.

"How about a drink at the rooftop restaurant?"

"Sure, fine!"

They had a drink and watched the sky beyond the glass-domed windows. They got to bed very late, then woke up very early and started with golf in the morning, tennis in the afternoon, and swimming in the early evening.

Amber could barely stand by the time they made it back to their hotel. She was half-asleep and the last in line as they entered their hallway and neared the room.

She was startled when Josie let out a wild scream. "What is it? Josie, what—"

She thought at first that her friend had been attacked, but it wasn't anything like that. Josie was in the arms of a tall man, and it took Amber only a second to realize that it was Josie's husband, Jim Bainbridge.

"Amber, Myra," he said, acknowledging the others, then grinned at his wife.

"What are you doing here?" Josie insisted. "You're supposed to be in Washington."

"I know, I know," Jim Bainbridge said. "But things are really slow right now, so I thought it would be nice if I went on that cruise Ted Larkspur was talking about. I decided to come and see if I couldn't collect a bevy of beauties to accompany me. What do you say? We could have another few days here, then fly down to Miami, spend a night and take off the next morning."

"I don't know—" Amber said.

"Well, I do! A cruise sounds like fun," Myra said. "And George is in England for at least another three weeks. Come on, Amber. If those two are together, we can share a cabin. Why not?"

"What do you say?" Jim asked her cheerfully.

She felt her throat go suddenly dry as she realized that she had seen Michael Adams near Senator

Daldrin. Maybe he had been hired as security for the senator.

"Come on, Amber!"

Why not? She wanted to go. She wanted to see Michael Adams again, and she had a strange feeling that he would be on the cruise.

"I . . ."

"Come on, Amber!" they all said in unison.

"All right!" she agreed. "But only if you and Jim go off and get your own room and leave Myra and me to go to sleep right now. My feet are killing me!"

"I've already gotten a room," Jim assured her. "I was just trying to collect my wife."

"Well, collect her and go, huh?" Myra said.

Thirty minutes later the Bainbridges were gone, and Amber had showered and lain down in her bed, her weary feet up on a pillow, her eyes closed.

But as exhausted as she was, she didn't sleep. Little flames of excitement were burning within her. She knew, with certainty, that the man with the ice-blue eyes and searing touch would be on that cruise.

She was a fool to be going. . . .

No . . . she really had no choice.

Chapter 5

The ship was called the *Alexandria*, and she was new and beautiful, but she didn't compare to the color of the sunset as they left land behind them and started out of the channel.

Amber stood by the ship's rail and watched the colors reflected on the water and blazing in the sky. They'd reached Miami last night, but they had yet to join up with Senator Daldrin's party. They had gone to Bayside for dinner, then spent the day shopping, and it had been just about time for the ship to sail when they had made it aboard.

Amber had dropped her belongings quickly in the stateroom she and Myra would be sharing—a large, beautiful room—and had run out. The others had been close behind her, but since she had been anxious to watch the ship's departure, she had left them behind to hurry along the rail. She loved everything about the water, the soft mist that seemed to hang in the air, the fresh, clean, salty smell of the sea. And there was a nice breeze to combat the tail end of the brutal June sun. Her hair was lifted from her shoulders as she stood there, and the soft wisps drifted lightly against her flesh. She wore a soft striped cotton halter dress, and the breeze picked up the hem of her skirt and sent it flying against her.

As they moved through the channel, the fingertip islands and roads of Miami and then Miami Beach slowly disappeared. The sun fell lower against the horizon, and the pinks in the sky gave way to shades of gray. Amber liked standing on the deck, feeling the breeze, feeling the sea. The air seemed to settle over her softly and soothingly. She could reflect on her life here, she thought. On her years with Peter, on the future that lay before her. There was nothing like the endlessness of the sea. She closed her eyes and lifted her face to the sky and cherished the air against her cheeks.

''What the hell are you doing on this ship?''

The quick, harsh question brought her whirling quickly around.

Michael Adams was indeed on the ship. He was standing not two feet from her in dark jeans and a dark T-shirt, sneakers on his feet, his hair unruly in the breeze, his hands on his hips and his gaze a heated fire. There was such low fury in the question that for a moment she caught her breath, wishing she had never come.

Then she lifted her chin. It was a free world.

"Cruising, Mr. Adams. That's what I'm doing."

"Does your father know where you are?"

A guilty little pang seized her. Actually, he didn't. She'd been trying to get through to him all week, but all she'd managed to do was tell his various secretaries and assistants that she would try again. She'd finally written him a letter yesterday. But it hadn't really mattered. He didn't expect her back for a while.

But just what was that to Michael Adams?

"Mr. Adams, that's really none of your business. I assure you, I'm quite old enough to make my own decisions."

"He doesn't know you're here!" His words were harsh, and Amber felt as if a whole new atmosphere had settled over the deck. They were alone in the growing darkness—others who had waved goodbye to the shore had given up their vigil and gone in to change for dinner, or relax in one of the lounges, or perhaps just amble around. The salt-sea air seemed to change around them, razor sharp, touched by electricity. She wanted to slap the man, but she wanted to walk closer and touch him, too. He would be alive with fury, trembling, hot.

She was shivering, alternating between hot and cold. It was all very ridiculous; in the whole of her life, she'd never felt the way he made her feel, and she didn't like the lack of control one bit. He thought she shouldn't be on the ship; that much was obvious. But she wasn't going to kowtow to some two-bit security officer—no matter how much he thought of himself.

"Will you excuse me, Mr. Adams?" she said, and she was very proud of the sound of her voice; it was cool and controlled and level. She started to walk by him with the same disciplined disdain, but her exit was ruined when he caught her arm and whirled her around to face him.

They were touching. His hand lay on her arm, and she could tell that he was just as she had thought he would be: hot, vibrant, trembling just slightly, tense and electric.

"Answer me. Your father doesn't know you're aboard this ship, does he?"

She swallowed, finding it difficult to meet his eyes. She stared down to where his fingers wound around her arm in a vise. He wasn't hurting her, but she could not have moved, not unless he chose to let her go. She met his eyes at last and wondered what had happened to him to make him so very cold, and yet so fiercely hot, all in one. She didn't know. She was aware only that she was in over her head with this man and that she should keep her distance, no matter how much he intrigued her.

She didn't tug on her arm. She wasn't about to appear undignified. "If you wouldn't mind, Mr. Adams, I'd like to get by."

"I mind. Who are you here with?"

She sighed with great patience, her teeth grating. "Congressman Bainbridge and his wife, and Myra Norman. Shouldn't you be elsewhere? I assume that, if you're here, you're gainfully employed in some capacity. Now, will you please remove your hand from my arm?''

To her amazement, he released her abruptly, turned around and left the deck.

Amber discovered that she was shaking so badly that she had to sink into one of the deck chairs. It was several long moments before she could stand up again.

Myra wasn't in their stateroom when Amber finally mustered up the strength to reach it. She showered and dressed for dinner. They were scheduled for the second seating, she knew, but once she was dressed she was too restless to remain in the stateroom. The casino was straight down from their room, and she found herself walking in that direction.

Along the hallway she passed a pair of handsomely dressed children of about ten and eight, the boy in a dinner suit, the girl in an elegant pink lace dress, with socks to match. Despite their appearance, the brother was chasing the sister mercilessly down the hall, and the sister charged right into Amber. The girl backed away, horrified, and looked around quickly to see if her parents had noticed the offense, but they were nowhere to be seen. She stared at Amber with her mouth very round. "I—I'm sorry!" she stuttered.

Amber smiled and shook her head. "It's all right." She looked over the girl's head to her brother. "But you should be careful, you know. There may be some real grouches on board this ship."

The girl nodded, smiling. Then she tried to don a very serious expression. "We'll be careful, I promise." She kept staring at Amber, and she smiled again. "You're pretty."

Amber laughed. "Thank you. So are you."

The little boy was behind his sister then, taking her arm. "Thanks, miss. Come on, Arabella." They hurried past her. Amused, Amber watched them go. When she turned again, her heart slammed hard against her chest. Michael Adams was there, ahead of her, standing by the case where the boarding pictures were being displayed. He had changed for dinner, too. He wasn't as elegant as he had been in his tuxedo, but he was every bit as striking. He was in black again, and he was watching her with a curious light in his eyes.

Amber squared her shoulders and started past him. "Good evening, Mr. Adams," she said, brushing by.

"Miss Larkspur."

He said nothing more as she passed him, and a curious feeling of disappointment fell over her.

She entered the casino and watched the handsomely dressed men and women at the blackjack tables for a while, then bought herself a handful of quarters for the slot machines. She idly tossed in coins and watched as watermelons and little black lines refused to line up. Frustrated, she turned.

Michael Adams was leaning against the next machine. She wondered uncomfortably just how long he had been there, and she instinctively knew that he had been watching her for quite a while. Instantly, her temper flared, and she was on the defensive. "I am old enough to gamble, Mr. Adams."

"So I imagine," he said.

When she started to turn away, he stepped closer. "Giving up so easily?"

She paused. His voice was light. There was an almost teasing quality to it.

"I've fed that machine quite enough, I think."

"Oh, I don't know. Loyalty seems to pay off most of the time." He slipped a quarter into the machine. It whizzed and whined, and to Amber's complete annoyance, the bars with the little money signs in the middle all lined up neatly. The machine began to clang and chirp, and quarters seemed to spill out by the dozens.

She looked from the quarters to Michael Adams. He was smiling at her, ignoring his winnings.

"Congratulations," she said.

"I just put that quarter in for you."

She shook her head. "I don't want your money."

"Well, I don't want yours."

"Hey, lady!" said a fat man with a cigar. "I'll take your quarters!"

"There's about fifty dollars there. What say we hand it over to a charity, then?" Michael suggested.

The tension left her. She suddenly found herself smiling, too. "All right." She named her favorite charity.

"Sounds good," Michael said.

Amber looked at the fat man. "Could I borrow one of your cups, please?"

"Sure, lady. Sure."

Once she had cashed in the coins, she turned around to find that the changeable Michael Adams was waiting for her. "I think it's time for dinner," he told her.

"Oh? Are we dining together?"

"Very together." She looked up at him. He was staring straight ahead as they walked down the hall, his hand on her elbow. "Myra managed the seating arrangements. We're all at the senator's table."

Leave it to matchmaking Myra, Amber thought. She was married, but Michael Adams was young and unattached, and so was Amber.

It was what she had wanted, wasn't it? Amber thought. But she didn't know. The more she saw of Michael, the less it seemed that she could ever know or understand him. One moment he beckoned to her; the next he thrust her away. Far, far away.

"Where do you live?" he asked her as they started down the stairs to the dining room.

"Now?"

His brow arched. "Do you live different places at different times?"

"Do you?"

"Yes," he answered flatly. "And you?"

"I've just moved back to Washington."

"From where?"

"Atlanta."

"Um," he said, but there was something about the way he said it.

"And what does that mean?"

"It means you've just come from some great and traumatic relationship. Be careful on the rebound, Miss Larkspur."

"I'm not on the rebound."

"I'll bet you are." He stopped walking suddenly. They were at the foot of the stairs, and he swung toward her, one foot on the bottom step, the bulk of his body preventing her from further movement. "They say that most women need a quick and careless affair after something like that. Just someone to clean away the past. Someone they may not even care to know well, but someone who attracts them on the most basic level. It shouldn't be me. I'm warning you—it shouldn't be me."

Amber was nearly speechless. "What!" she snapped.

"I said—"

She shoved him, her hands planted firmly upon his chest. He moved, giving way for her. "Amber, I'm trying—"

"Don't try!" she retorted, her chin high as she headed toward the dining room. There were no lines at the doorway. The second-seating passengers must have already entered. Good. She could walk in with dignity and ignore Michael Adams.

No...she couldn't.

She stopped and swung around. "I should warn you. I find you to be one of the most obnoxious men I've ever met, and it's really a pity that your worth can't possibly measure up to your ego. I'm not on the rebound, I am not looking for an affair, and I most assuredly have no desire to go to bed with you."

They were close. They weren't touching, but they were close. She felt the curious ice and fire of his eyes upon her as if he was touching her.

He smiled slowly. Ruefully. "That's good," he said softly. "Because I *do* want to go to bed with *you*, and it would be a mistake. A horrible mistake."

He walked past her and into the dining room. Amber stood still for several seconds, shocked by his admission.

Then she wanted to scream. She was tired of him delivering his curt, crude and commanding statements—then walking on and leaving her standing.

She swung around again, determined to maintain her composure. She entered the dining room, and a maître d' was quickly at her side. She asked for Senator Daldrin's table and was quickly escorted to it.

The table was full, except for her place, which was beside Adams. The men all stood for her arrival. Adams pulled out her chair politely while the others greeted her.

She thanked him equally politely and sat. She felt the whisper of his breath against her cheek as he pushed in her chair.

"Amber, it's good to see you," Ian Daldrin said as he buttered a roll. She looked across the table at him. The senator was smiling, but she felt that his words were a lie. He wasn't glad to see her, not at all. What was going on here?

"Thank you, Senator."

"Does your father know you're here?"

She gritted her teeth in silence and swallowed hard before answering. "I'm not sure if he does or doesn't. It depends on whether or not he got my letter." There was wine on the table. Michael Adams was filling her glass.

"I see," the senator said. What did he see?

"We didn't intend to come at all!" Josie was explaining. She smiled adoringly at Jim. "We were all set to spend two full weeks on land when Jim appeared, and the offer seemed just too good to be true."

"Great, Jim, really great," Daldrin mumbled.

"I didn't think I could get away at first," Jim said.

"Well, we're all here now," Ian Daldrin said, picking up his menu. "Oh, Amber, you have met this young man beside you, I take it?"

"We met in Washington, at a party," Amber said.

"Did you? Well, good. Let's take a look at this menu, shall we? Swordfish, grouper, dolphin, lobster tails, lamb chops, steaks. We've got quite a choice here, eh?"

It wasn't long before the dinner conversation turned to politics and quickly became lively. Then it started becoming heated and too lively.

Finally Ian Daldrin cleared his throat and tossed his napkin on the table. "Well, enough of this!" he announced cheerfully to all of them. "I'm on vacation." He came around to Amber, pulled out her chair. "Would you care to dance with an old friend? I can't take the disco. Too old for that, I'm afraid. But

I hear they have a nice dance band in the Neptune Lounge.''

He might not want her aboard for his own strange reasons, and he was one of her father's oldest friends, but since she was there he was going to treat her politely. She smiled up at him. "Certainly."

He escorted her along several hallways, down a flight of stairs and into the lounge. There was a good dance band there, and in the senator's arms she whirled around to a number of songs. He mentioned that their first port of call would be a private island in the Bahamas, that only the *Alexandria* had privileges there, and that motor launches would take them to the barren beaches, if they so desired.

"Sounds like heaven," Amber assured him.

"You want to be alone?"

"With endless stretches of white beach and warm water? Yes!"

"Well, don't go off alone. Anywhere."

"Why?"

"Because it might not be safe. Really, Amber. Don't go off alone."

Alone? Amber thought. All she wanted was to avoid Michael Adams. She would wake up bright and early, don her suit and gather her gear, then take off in the first launch. If Myra or Josie wanted to come along, fine, but she wasn't going to have her vacation ruined by that irritating man.

"I'll be careful," she promised.

He led her off the floor. The others were grouped around two tables. Michael Adams was smoking a cigarette, talking politely with Josie, but Amber felt that he had been watching her and the senator too closely.

"Michael, I'm winded," Ian said. "Take over for an old man, will you?"

Amber wanted to crawl beneath the table. She felt the color flood her cheeks. "Actually, I think I'll call it a day, Senator—"

"I'd be delighted, Miss Larkspur."

He was up, and seconds later they were on the floor. His hands were on her, and she was wondering how he could make such an incredibly intimate thing out of dancing. He had taken her quickly into his arms at the senator's suggestion, but now that they were out on the floor, he seemed angry again. Her fingers brushed his lapel, and after several long seconds of silence she looked into his eyes.

"Damn you," he told her, a ragged edge to his voice, the words deep and fierce. "Damn you!"

She moistened her lips, frightened by his tone. "I don't know what you're so mad at."

"You know exactly what I'm mad at."

"Don't dance with me, then. Don't touch me. Don't come near me."

"We're with the same party. You're hard to avoid."

"So are you."

"I told you to take care."

"Yes, yes, you've given me fair warning. And I'm just fine. I have no intention of throwing myself at your feet."

"Don't you?"

The question was harsh. And then he was leading her off the floor, but he wasn't taking her to the table, he was leading her out of the lounge and onto the deck, where the darkness descended upon them despite the ship's lights, where the wind whipped at them and they were alone. Where she found herself pressed against the ship's railing, his arms around her. He was kissing her again, kissing her as savagely as he had that first time. She wanted desperately to deny him, but she couldn't. She met the passion of his kiss, her arms tightening around him, her fingers feeling the ripple of hard muscle beneath his jacket and clothing. Then she touched his face, his hair. And his hand moved over her, cupping her breast, sliding along her midriff to her hip, his fingers teasing the stockinged flesh of her thighs as they slipped with no question or apology beneath her hem. They could make love right there, she thought wildly. It could be his intention to press her ever closer to the rail and thrust up her skirt and end the friction then and there, and in mounting horror she wondered if she hated him for it or desired him all the more.

It didn't matter. A small sound escaped her lips, and he pulled away from her, dropping her hem, staring at her wide, dilated eyes.

"For the love of God, stay away from me," he warned her, and she knew he was going to turn and walk away again.

"No!" She practically shrieked the word. He paused, startled, and Amber rushed past him, turning only once to say, "For the love of God, *you* stay away from *me*!"

She ran inside. The brilliance of the light nearly blinded her at first, but she hurried to the stairs, found her deck and raced for her stateroom. Once inside, she slammed the door, leaned against it and breathed deeply.

It was going to be a wretched, wretched night.

Myra had no interest in waking up early to seek out a quiet and deserted beach. Amber didn't mind going alone—it was a good opportunity to reflect on what she was going to do with her life.

She dressed silently in an ebony French-cut two-piece with a high waist and string ties. Over it she wore a huge T-shirt. In sneakers and a straw hat and sunglasses, with a bag holding lotion, a bottle of mineral water and towels, she was ready. She was one of the first on deck at seven-thirty. The launches wouldn't be ready for another few minutes, but coffee was being served at the buffet, and she took a cup with her to the rail and looked toward the island. It was beautiful, all overgrown, with no buildings, no cement, nothing except for the foliage and nearly snow-white sand that seemed to stretch forever.

"Morning, Amber."

She spun around. Senator Daldrin was already up. In swim trunks, he seemed in very good shape for a man of his age. Not an ounce of extra flesh fell over his waistband.

"Good morning, Senator."

"You weren't planning on going off alone, now, were you?"

"I'm just heading out to the island." The deck wasn't empty any longer. A few other members of his party were milling around. And if the senator was up, Amber was sure that her nemesis was around, too.

He was. She saw him sitting at a table. He was wearing swim trunks and an open shirt, his eyes hidden beneath the dark lenses of his glasses. He lifted his hand, acknowledging her.

Damn.

She looked at Daldrin. "Senator, I'm almost thirty."

"Are you? Doesn't seem like so many years could have passed. I've known you since you were a little thing, you know."

"But I'm not little anymore. I swim like a fish, and I would really like some privacy today. Please understand."

"Oh, I understand." He smiled and walked away from her. A moment later he paused by the table where Michael Adams was nursing his coffee. The senator said something, and the other man nodded.

Irritated, Amber turned away. Within moments the launches were ready. It would have been churlish to avoid Senator Daldrin to such an extent that she refused to ride in his launch, so she willingly went along with the party, sitting on the seat right in front of him.

The motor hummed to life, and a young Hispanic crewman steered the small craft toward the island, shouting above the roar of the motor. "Last boat goes back at eight this evening, *sí*, people? You be careful, you have fun, but you be careful, and make it back to the ship, eh? We'll have beer and soda and rumrunners here on the beach, and you're not going to be driving, so you can have a good time. Just don't get lost!''

Someone chuckled, and there was a rush of conversation. Amber was startled when she realized that she was sitting behind Michael Adams, and that another man was whispering to him.

''It's not tonight, I tell you. When the time is right, I will know.''

''You're certain.''

''I am certain.''

Amber leaned forward, anxious to hear more of the conversation, but they had both fallen silent.

The launch made its way through the shallow waters, spray rising up around them, to the shore. The crewmen jumped out, dragging the launch up on the sand. Amber was quick to leap out unassisted, but before she had taken two steps, Senator Daldrin was beside her.

''Amber, come on, spend some time with us.''

She opened her mouth to explain that she just wanted to be alone for a while when she received unexpected assistance from Michael Adams. ''Senator, nothing could possibly go wrong today. I'm sure Miss Larkspur will be all right.''

Ian Daldrin threw up his hands. ''Bless you then, and have a great day.''

She gave him a quick kiss on the cheek and hurried off. Others were already scurrying along the sand, trying to find their own little nook or cranny of privacy along the stretch of beach. If she didn't hurry, she wouldn't find a place.

Fifteen minutes later, she was still walking. Others had already chosen their little plots of paradise, and she had to keep going and going to find her own patch of pristine beach. It didn't matter; she felt a curious rush of energy that morning, despite the lack of sleep she'd experienced lately. She didn't mind walking at all. What she really wanted to do was run and run and run, until the tension was gone, and the energy, too, and all the ragged confusion of emotion.

In another ten minutes she paused. She was far beyond the other bathers from the ship, but the walk had been well worth it. She had come upon a cove with high dunes and rock formations on either side, with scattered foliage and pines eking out a desperate existence to give the exquisite little beach in between just the right amount of sun and shade. Nothing marred the sand, not a soda bottle nor a gum wrapper; there wasn't a single sign of human habitation. There was just the beach, the sun, the sky and the water, turquoise as she had never seen turquoise before.

Right away she dropped her beach bag and took off her hat, sneakers, T-shirt and glasses, then raced for the water. It was beautiful, even exquisite! The day was hot, but the water was still cool from the night, and it seemed to awaken and refresh and cleanse her. She dove deep, then surfaced and struck out hard with a crawl before turning toward shore with the back-stroke. She swam as she had walked, with determination and explosive energy, and then at last she went to the shallows and rose and started walking toward the beach again.

She stopped, staring toward the sand. She wasn't alone in her Eden anymore, that much was for sure. Michael Adams had found her. He was shirtless and barefoot now, and it was the first time she had seen his shoulders and chest. He looked just as she had imagined he would. He was in better shape than a man who simply went to a gym. His belly was taut and trim and rippled with muscle. He was lean all over, but still taut muscles bulged in his arms, his shoulders, his tawny-dusted, coppery chest. There were scars on him, too, several that she could see. A long one across his right shoulder. Another along his side.

She stared at him for a moment, then started walking again, angrily. She realized that he was soaking wet when she strode past him, but this was a beach and he was supposed to be wet, so she didn't think anything of it. She reach down for her bag, pulled out her towel, then turned in fury. "'Stay away from me, Miss Larkspur!'" she mimicked. "I'm trying very hard to do just that! What the hell are you doing on my beach!"

"It isn't exactly your beach."

"I walked long and hard to find it, and I think I made it clear that I wanted to be alone."

"I wanted you to be alone, too, Miss Larkspur, but I'm afraid your friend the senator had other ideas."

"I thought you were supposed to be guarding him?"

"Maybe you shouldn't think so much."

"Maybe you shouldn't take your work quite so seriously—and leave me alone!" Amber spread out her towel and reached for her sunglasses, trying not to allow him to see just how shaken she was. It had been a mistake, she realized. She shouldn't have tried to escape. She should have stayed with the others, with people. It was dangerous to be alone with him.

Definitely dangerous.

"Why, you damn brat!" He was dripping on her. Standing over her and dripping on her. "You scared me half to death, staying under that long! I dove like crazy, sure you were drowning, and then you came waltzing back in with a mouthful of wisecracks!"

She sat up, stripping off her glasses, staring at him furiously. "No one asked you to come!"

"Even good swimmers drown!"

"But I wanted to be alone."

"You have no sense, but there are people who still care about you. My God, I feel like—"

He broke off. Amber stumbled quickly to her feet, facing him. "You feel like what? Go on, tell me, spit it out. Don't hesitate. Really."

"All right, I *won't* hesitate!" he shouted, reaching for her. She had no idea what his intention was, and she didn't want to find out. With a screech, she turned to run.

There was no one to hear her on her private beach, in her protected cove, her Eden. Her bare feet hit the white sand, sending it flying. The foliage dipped and swayed, scattering the sunbeams as she ran.

And as she fell.

His arm swept around her bare midriff, and his weight bore them down into the sand, where he loomed over her, his hands on her shoulders, his legs straddling her. And he was yelling again, telling her that she was a fool, her father's spoiled little darling, and that if she had any sense at all, she would learn to be more careful.

She slammed her fist against his chest. "I've managed very nicely for nearly thirty years, thank you very much. Now get off me, you gorilla!"

"Amber, you don't—"

He broke off. He was staring at her. His hands fell suddenly from her shoulders, and his fingers entwined with hers. They both looked at the soft white of her slender hand and the darker, rugged bronze of his, and then he slowly lowered their hands to the sand together. And as he did so, he lowered his face to hers. She knew that he was going to kiss her again, and she found herself bracing for the violence.

But there was none. Today, when his lips touched hers, it seemed as if they had no more force than a breath. Flickers of warmth, of wetness, touched her as he teased the rim of her lips with the tip of his tongue. Then he moaned and wrapped her in his arms, and suddenly they were rolling into the sand. When he kissed her again, it was the deep, never-ending kiss she had come to know, the fusion of life and soul, the touch of fire that entered through her lips but coiled in her belly. He held her face and kissed her more slowly, more deeply. And then he just held her there in the sand, and his groan touched her ear. "This isn't right."

It wasn't right, and she knew it. She had touched something forbidden, but she knew that she couldn't walk away. She moved against him, her fingers brushing through his damp hair, moving over his nape. The back of his hand brushed her cheek, her eyes met his, and they both knew that there was no denial within them. He lowered his hand to her breast, peeling away the black bandanna bra to bare her fullness to his touch. His palm grazed over her, rotating around her nipple, and eliciting a sharp sound from her. But she didn't look away from him, and he spoke again, angry with her, with himself.

"Don't you understand? I have nothing to give you. Nothing at all." But his hand shook when he touched her.

She had no reply for him, only a soft cry that escaped her as she arched against his touch, and perhaps that was the reply he needed, for his lips sought hers, sliding down against her skin, tasting the sea salt on her body. His tongue teased over her throat; then his mouth closed over her breast, sucking the nipple deep within, his tongue swirling slowly, provocatively around it.

He had found the strings of her suit, and she was freed from the black top, leaving his hands and the wet stroking of his tongue to move over her with no restraint. The sun was hot, the sand gritty, and they were both covered with the salt sheen of the ocean, but none of that seemed to matter as he made love to her.

Passion entered his touch. It was not that the tenderness left it; it was that something fierce and desperate entered again. He was no hesitant lover; having chosen his course, he touched her where he would, his fingers slipping beneath her bikini bottoms, peeling them away. And as he peeled the damp fabric away from her, his lips followed the nakedness of her flesh, tasting her belly, and below, his hair brushing her flesh, his breath touching her, on fire with the day. He shifted her weight, stripping the bottoms from her completely, and she thought that he would be swift then, too hungry to wait. And yet he was not.

She opened her eyes and discovered he was staring at her. But when her eyes met his with wonder, he rose quickly and shed his bathing trunks. The breath left her as he came down to her again, and she surveyed the man, her heart pulsing, her body trembling. Bending over her, he found her lips. He stroked her throat with his tongue, then moved leisurely downward over her body again, just touching her breasts with the same damp stroke, his hand playing along her hip as he did so. Finally his fingers moved between her thighs, touching her lightly at first, then touching her more deeply. His kiss fell against her abdomen, her thighs, and then he watched for a long moment before his head fell lower against her, before she felt a slow, intimate stroking that invaded every cell in her being and ignited a desire hotter than the blaze of the sun. A cry tore from her, and then she was

in his arms, looking into his eyes again, and she felt
the tip of his desire throbbing at the threshold of her
own. He pulled her close, stroking her hair, and he
whispered that she should wrap her legs around him,
and when she did, he thrust into her.

She heard the ocean, the sound of the waves, the cry
of a bird high overhead. But she wondered whether the
cry might not be her own, for she felt nothing then but
the power of the man, entering her, stroking again and
again, shattering everything she had thought she knew
of life, taking her with a passion that was both violent and tender, and with a wanting that was as never-
ending as the darkness of the sea at night. Her fingers
dug into muscle and sinew, and she bit his shoulder,
feeling the sensations grow, feeling his shuddering
power deep within her, harder, faster, nearly unbearable. And then she once more felt the sun, the sand,
the breeze that caressed her. She cried out again as a
climax burst through her, and he moved again, so deep
inside her that she thought they were one. Suddenly he
fell down beside her, the wind rushing around them,
the sand gritty and soft beneath them.

Neither spoke for the longest time. And then Amber felt like a fool, or worse, and she sat up, embar-
rassedly trying to cover herself while she looked for the
pieces of her bathing suit. And then he reached out
and touched her.

"What are you doing now?" he asked impatiently,
and when her eyes gave her answer, he shook his head
and touched her chin. "You're beautiful," he said almost harshly. "Please don't act like that."

She wasn't sure whether she was angry or hurt. It didn't matter. She stood stark naked and made no attempt to hide herself—it was too late; the horse had certainly already run out of the barn—and then she snatched up her bathing suit. She started toward the water, but he followed her, swinging her around to face him. "So now you're going to be upset. Damn it, don't! You're beautiful, you're warm, you're wonderful. Too wonderful. Too...innocent."

"Are you through?" she asked him.

"Amber, I'm sorry. I told you I had nothing to give—"

"What makes you think you have anything I want?"

She saw his jaw tighten. "I see. Maybe you *did* need a little fling. Maybe you *were* out looking for an affair, and the man, the caring, the warmth, didn't matter."

She stopped, and the anger and everything else drained away from her. "I didn't want an affair," she said softly. "I just wanted you."

Then she raced for the water, anxious to dive into it, to feel it around her, refreshing and cleansing her.

Chapter 6

Adam watched her run into the water, watched the sway of her hips. Her movements fascinated him, brought new life to him. And he watched the straightness of her spine, the square set of her shoulders, the tilt of her chin. He swore softly beneath his breath and felt a tightening within him, and he wanted to give himself a solid kick, except that that wouldn't do any good, either.

She wasn't anything like Sonia. Sonia had been small, compact, lushly curved, with dark eyes and rippling dark hair. Amber Larkspur was tall and slender, a woman who seemed to flow beneath his touch. She was blond, and her eyes were the color of the sea, sometimes blue and sometimes green, and sometimes startling shades in between. And he never, never should have touched her, and he'd damn well known it, but he'd touched her anyway. Now things were churning inside, because it seemed like some kind of betrayal, as if he had forgotten Sonia, as if he had forgotten love. And that seemed stupid, too, because there had been other women. There just hadn't been another woman like Amber. He hadn't wanted anyone the way he had wanted her....

And it had never felt so good to have a woman. He'd known how she would be, so giving, so fluid, so alive and intense in her lovemaking. Long before he had touched her, he had known that she would feel like silk, that she would move with the undulating beauty of the waves. And he had thought that she was a beautiful woman the first time he had seen her, but it hadn't been her beauty that had drawn him; beauty was not so rare a quality. He had liked her smile when the rambunctious kids had plowed into her, and he had liked the sound of her laughter; it had seemed to touch some fragile nerve within him. Most of all he had liked the way her eyes met his, always challenging. No matter what he said to her, she listened and replied with a startling honesty; she couldn't be cowed, and neither did she seem to play games. She had moved far out into the water now, and he thought he knew what she was trying to do, to let the salt and sea and the coolness slide over her, and wash away the startling heat that had burst between them. But her bikini still lay on the shore, and he could see glimpses of her bare flesh beneath the turquoise waters, and no sense of his own betrayal regarding either Sonia or the life that he lived could still the excitement that grew within him again. It was wrong, terribly wrong. In a matter of days he would be gone, out of her life. He would slip away with the kidnappers and Daldrin, and he would be out of her life completely. He wouldn't come back, because he wasn't the right man to come back; he lived with violence, and he expected to die with violence. Once it would have mattered; once he had wanted more, much more. But that had been before Sonia died. He lived a dangerous lie each day now, for it seemed he was constantly discovering more of Ali Abdul's men aboard the *Alexandria*, men who watched him because he hadn't fully earned their trust. He wouldn't know until the last moment when the higher echelon of the Death Squad would be coming for Daldrin, and the waiting was tense and hard. But the moment would come. It would come soon.

But not today.

He stared out at the water and reminded himself that he was in love with a dead woman, that he had nothing to give to Amber Larkspur, that he'd had no right to touch her, and he sure as hell had no right to touch her again.

His feet started moving anyway. She wasn't a kid, and he'd been honest with her. And she'd been honest in return. Whatever the chemistry was, it had touched her, too. She had wanted him. And anything that had felt so right and so fulfilling just couldn't be completely wrong.

His feet touched the water.

Within moments he was up to his waist, and then he was swimming toward her. She was floating on her back, but she sensed when he came near, and she stood, the waterline just above her breasts, the waves barely covering the large, dusky-rose nipples. He stood apart from her for a long moment, and her eyes searched his; then she smiled slowly. "We're not doing a very good job of staying away from one another," she said.

"No," he replied. Her hair, sleek and wet, was drawn away from her face, and the clean lines of her throat and shoulders and breasts were achingly evident. His voice softened, and he was surprised at the tremor in it, the touch of tenderness. "You said you wanted me. Me, as an individual man. And not because of convenience, but because when we met, certain . . . feelings arose."

"I didn't say all that, but yes," she whispered. "It's what I meant."

"Come here." He spoke commandingly, his tone harsh, and he thought she would ignore him.

But she didn't.

She moved through the water, coming so close that her breasts brushed his chest and he could feel the softness of her. He pulled her into his arms and held her, his mouth covering hers, and he tasted the salt and the sea and the sweetness that was uniquely this woman. He kissed her more deeply and felt her tremble, felt the rise of his passion against her belly. He planted his feet hard in the sand and drew her more tightly to him as he raised his lips from hers at last and looked into her eyes.

They were wide and luminous, reflecting the waves and the elusive colors of the water. He dipped his head again and kissed her throat, and his tongue traced a watery trail to her collarbone. He felt the trembling of her body again and cupped her breast, feeling the hardness of the nipple. "I do want you," he whispered to her.

She seemed to melt against him. "Here?" she whispered.

His eyes met hers again. "Here. Yes. Right here. Now, in the water." He teased his fingers along her thigh, stroking her intimately with his thumb, creating a bold rhythm. And he whispered against her ear, "Now, Amber. Here, now."

She moistened her lips with her tongue, and he lifted her and told her to wrap her legs around him, then guided her down onto him and held her tight. His hands slid low over the roundness of her buttocks, and he lifted her against him again and again, bringing her down hard, letting the rhythm, the pace, increase until she felt as hot as the sun despite the coolness of the water. Her breasts stroked his chest with every movement, adding to the need within him. It rose and rose, hot and sweet, and everything within him tensed and constricted, and then a cry burst from him, and his seed spilled into her. She, too, cried out, but softly, her arms wrapped around him, her head burrowing against his shoulder.

He held her that way for endless moments, until the water felt cool again.

Then she lifted her head, and her eyes met his. "We should get dressed. This isn't really a private beach."

He nodded and slowly released her, even though he didn't want to. She swam with clean strokes to the beach. He waited, watching as she picked up the pieces of her black bathing suit and slipped into them. She stared down the beach for a moment, then retrieved his trunks and came to the water's edge. There was nothing hurried about her movements, nothing of regret or shame.

"The senator is walking our way," she said quietly and tossed out his trunks.

Daldrin. Adam wondered what the man would have thought if he had decided on his jaunt a few minutes earlier.

He stepped into his trunks and walked out of the water. "Hey, there you two are!" Ian Daldrin called out. There was a note of relief in his voice, as if they had been gone a long time. Had they? Adam wondered.

"Senator," Amber drawled, "you must have known that I'd be all right. After all, you sent Mr. Adams to keep an eye on me, I'm certain."

"Well, maybe I did," Ian admitted.

"And as you can see, we're just fine," she went on.

"Yes, yes, but you should come back. They're serving lunch, a barbecue in the sand. The calypso band is playing. And they make a damn good rumrunner.'' He offered Amber his arm. She took it without looking at Adam.

But Daldrin did look back, and there was puzzlement in his eyes as he studied the younger man.

Adam followed them in silence. He couldn't see why Daldrin was confused. It all seemed pretty obvious to him.

They ate hamburgers and hot dogs and sipped rumrunners on the shore.

Amber was amazed that she found it so easy to sit beside Senator Daldrin on her towel, to chat and to sip her drink as if her life hadn't just changed monumentally. She should be pondering her sins, she thought, and she wasn't.

Nor was she anywhere near Michael Adams. He had chosen a position in the sun behind them. He wore his dark glasses, and she couldn't see his eyes, so she couldn't even begin to attempt to fathom his thoughts.

But he was watching her, she knew. He was watching her, and he was watching Senator Daldrin. Sometimes he contributed to the conversation. He seemed to know Switzerland and Austria well, and his knowledge of British history was impressive. When he spoke, Amber felt a rush go through her, as if a cold river was washing over her. She had made love with a man she knew nothing about.

They watched the sunset from the shore, and it was beautiful. There was nothing to see as far as the eye could roam except for the ship and the sky and the horizon and the island, and it was all very beautiful, if just a bit forlorn.

Amber knew that she would never, ever forget the island.

They got back to the ship with just enough time to shower and change and go to dinner, but Amber didn't want to go to dinner. Instead she showered and donned a nightgown and curled up in bed, where she stared at the shadowed ceiling and wondered about everything she had done. Just thinking about him made her grow warm, made her breath come too quickly, and she could hear the hard pounding of her heart, and feel it in her breast. She should be ashamed of herself.

But she wasn't ashamed in the least. Whoever and whatever Michael Adams was, she just couldn't be ashamed. All the tempest between them had been leading straight to this, and it had been wonderful. She hoped that he didn't think she had stayed away from dinner because she was ashamed. She had stayed away, she realized, because she hadn't been alone all day, because she hadn't had a chance to savor and enjoy and relive the moments they had shared.

She couldn't sleep. After a while she rose and quickly donned a casual knit dress. She didn't bother with shoes, but left her cabin and walked on the deck. She had found a little island of privacy, she realized. An area where the lifeboats created deep shadows.

The night seemed like a black pit, like a void. All was silent except for the lapping of the waves against the ship and the muted sounds of the band coming from the lounge.

The moon suddenly came from behind a cloud. A full moon. It cast a soft glow over the water. I should be worrying about the rest of my life, she thought. And she thought, too, that she should be worrying about Peter. She had been there for him for so long. That had been the mistake. It wasn't a lack of caring; they had both cared, cared deeply. But she had been there to pick him up from his depressions when he should have been doing it himself, and maybe now he would learn to stand on his own and fulfill his potential.

Had she really wanted him to come after her, not so long ago? Yes, she probably had. The dream of marriage and children and Brownie meetings and Little League had been so strong. And now she didn't know what she wanted.

She knew she didn't really love Peter, not the way she'd thought she had. Not when she could be touched so deeply and so completely by a stranger. Not when she could revel in the intimacies they had shared. Not when she longed to share them again.

She heard a noise and turned. Farther down the deck she could see a man in a white suit. It was Daldrin. He had just lit a cigarette and was looking at the sea. Apparently he needed to be alone, too. To see the endless water and the darkness of the night.

She moved quietly into the shadows. Everyone needed a few moments alone, and there was nothing so alone as this.

But that wasn't quite true. She happened to glance toward the bow of the ship, where a set of stairs led up to the pool deck.

They weren't alone at all. Michael Adams was there, as silent as the night, watching either her or Daldrin.

He didn't back away or pretend not to see her. He spoke softly, but his voice carried down to her. "Good night, Amber."

She stared at him and called back, "Good night."

The breeze moved over her shoulders, and she shivered. He was still watching her as she stepped into the hallway and hurried to her cabin.

Nassau
June 14

Myra was decked out in something like a white tennis outfit with a huge straw hat perched atop her head and a massive white bag. "I intend to shop until I drop!" she informed Amber. "Are you coming?"

"Mmm, for a while," Amber agreed. "But I'm not as good a shopper as you are. I'll probably drop out after lunch and come back to the ship. Is that all right?"

"Of course, whatever you want. This is a vacation, remember?"

They could disembark right on shore as soon as the ship was cleared. The two women walked to the poolside, where a buffet was being served. Myra decided to prepare herself a plate. "All-out shopping can require strength, you know," she told Amber, who nodded and took a cup of coffee. They found an empty table and sat down. Myra munched on a strip of bacon, eyeing Amber. "Who are you looking for?" she asked.

"What?"

"Who are you looking for?"

"No one."

"Are you certain?"

"Of course. I was just watching everyone. People are so interesting."

"Oh, sure. People in general. I thought you might be looking for the intriguing Mr. Adams."

"No. Why should I be?"

"Because I think he was looking for you last night, at dinner. Not that he's obvious. Those eyes of his are so cold, yet I always get the feeling he's the kind of guy who burns hotter than fire. He's so wonderfully intense. So sexy. And I could have sworn you had noticed."

"He's interesting," Amber admitted. "Senator Daldrin must feel safe with him around."

"He ought to feel safe, because this ship is crawling with security."

"Is it?"

"You know it is. Very likely Daldrin will be president in another eight years. He's one of the most important men in the senate. In a sea of big fish, the man is a whale. You know that."

"I knew there was security," Amber murmured. She remembered the man talking to Michael Adams in the launch the other day. Was he security, too? Who knew? And who knew just exactly what Michael's position was?

Myra daintily cleaned her lips with her napkin and pulled out her compact to check her appearance, then smiled. "Shall we shop?"

"Sure."

Amber still hadn't seen Michael when they had disembarked and walked a good distance down Market Street. She bought her father an interesting carved head, then bought his housekeeper and herself some perfume. Myra had been serious about shopping until she dropped—her bag was already full with straw objects and T-shirts and all manner of souvenirs, including a clay pipe with a growling bear on it. "My husband will love it!" she proclaimed, defending her purchase.

"I didn't say a word," Amber told her.

At twelve they were about to stop for lunch when a pair of mopeds came up close behind them. They spun around. To Amber's amazement she saw Senator Daldrin on one of them, smiling like a little kid.

Michael Adams was behind him. Down the street was another group riding the little cycles. More security, she thought.

"How about lunch?" Daldrin inquired. "Have you eaten yet?"

"No, and we're just about famished!" Myra said. "What did you have in mind?"

"A little place up the road a piece. I came here with my wife, Katherine, a few years ago."

His wife had died less than two years earlier, and Amber knew that he still missed her deeply. Maybe it was important for him to go to the restaurant in her memory. She lifted her eyes past the senator. Michael's glasses were covering his eyes, but she felt warmth sweep over her anyway.

"How are we getting there?" Myra asked.

"Crawl on," Daldrin invited her.

"With you?" Myra asked incredulously.

"Yes. I know how to drive this thing quite well, thank you very much. Amber, get on with Michael. It will only take a few minutes."

It took more than a few minutes to get Myra on the moped with Ian and all her shopping bags. Amber sat behind Michael, her arms around his waist.

It was a nice place to be. She liked it.

When the moped took off, the wind whipped her hair around her face, so she buried it against his back.

"You all right?" he called to her.

"Perfect!" she returned. Yes, she was perfect. She breathed in his scent and felt little tremors invade her. The ride was too short. Within minutes she was getting off the moped, and she wasn't touching him anymore.

The place was a shack. "Best turtle soup in the world," Daldrin assured her. He led Myra up the steps. Amber felt Michael's hand on her back, and she followed Myra.

Inside, they sat together on a bench. Amber ordered a seafood stew and promised to taste the senator's turtle soup. Everyone ordered Bahamian beer and sat back to enjoy the soft, lazy atmosphere in the room.

They talked about food around the world, then they talked about places, then the conversation drifted toward the theater. Amber could feel Michael's thigh against her own. She sipped her beer and watched his hands. She liked his hands so much. They were large hands, lean, powerful. Looking at them, she remembered how they had felt on her skin.

She swallowed hard and stared at Myra, who had asked her a question she hadn't heard.

"Pardon?"

"I said, have you seen *Yellow Roses*?"

She flushed. "No, I, uh, what is it?"

"An off-off-Broadway show. It was wonderful, absolutely wonderful. And Michael has seen it, too."

She gazed at Michael. "I, uh, yes, I've seen it. I have a friend in the cast," he said.

"How wonderful." Myra launched into a long tribute to the show. Amber watched Michael and thought that he seemed uncomfortable—a different characteristic for him. Maybe she was imagining things. Maybe she was paying too much attention to his hands, or to the heat of his thigh.

When they had finished lunch, Daldrin and Michael drove them to the ship, then went to return the mopeds. Amber changed into a bathing suit and walked to the pool.

Late that afternoon, Michael finally appeared, but he didn't come near her. He lay across the pool from her, his dark glasses in place. He didn't seem to move much, except when he took a lazy dip in the pool, but she knew that no matter how at ease he seemed, he was always watching Daldrin.

And she thought he was watching her, too.

At sunset, he disappeared. Amber, annoyed at her disappointment, forced herself to stay out longer. Then she hurried to her stateroom and took a long shower, washed her hair and tried to pamper herself in every way imaginable. With fresh red polish on her fingernails and toenails, she dressed in an elegant black cocktail gown and started out of her cabin, certain that she would find someone she knew in the lounge.

She had barely reached the end of the quiet hallway when she heard a rushing sound behind her. She spun around, alarmed. A cabin door had opened.

Michael Adams was there in the hall, a large white ship's towel wrapped around his waist.

"Hi," he said.

She looked at his apparel. "Hi."

"Care to come in?"

"I'm not sure."

"Yes, you are."

His arm slipped around her, and she found herself inside his cabin, and in his arms. She pressed her lips against his bare chest and tasted the fresh-scrubbed texture there.

She was wonderfully, sweetly perfumed and powdered. He found the zipper of her gown and tugged it down, and the frothy material made a black pool at her feet. And then he stepped away, inhaling sharply, because the vision of her standing there was so erotic. She was wearing skimpy black panties and a matching low-cut lacy bra, garters, stockings and black heels.

He stepped toward her and found himself kneeling, his tongue teasing the bare flesh over the black lace of her panties, his fingers suddenly shaking. He backed her toward the bunk, his mouth fusing with hers, and when she lay down, he slipped her panties down her legs and pulled them away, discarding them heedlessly on the floor. She was even more erotic with the golden color of her flesh and the soft gold triangle at the juncture of her thighs highlighted by the black lace stockings. Her eyes were nearly closed, her thick lashes lying over her cheeks.

He parted her thighs and buried his face between them.

Her fingers tore into his hair, and soft, mewling sounds escaped her as she twisted violently, then began to move subtly against him, rising, falling. She whispered to him, but he knew no mercy as he caressed and teased the bud of her greatest desire. A light touch, a deep touch, a slide, a caress . . . time was endless; her motion was beautiful. She cried out, and he felt the flood of sweet nectar from her body, then rose high above her, impatiently discarding the towel that had been wrapped around his waist. He met her eyes and kissed her slowly and completely. He rose again and lifted the swell of her breasts from the encompassing black lace of her bra. He closed his mouth around her as he penetrated her body with his own, thrusting deeply, finding himself enclosed tightly, tightly sheathed. And then he began to move, and time and space and night suddenly knew no boundaries.

Eons later he lay silent beside her. They needed to get up; he had to be at dinner, but he couldn't quite bring himself to rise. The scent of her perfume was light on the air, and he didn't want to dispel it, and the feel of her body beside his was so damn good.

"Michael?"

He didn't answer. For a moment he had forgotten that was his name.

"Michael?" She was up on one elbow, her hair tumbling in waves over her face, and she seemed incredibly blond and pure and innocent and beautiful. "Where are you from?"

He closed his fingers around hers. "Around." He rose, pushing her head to the pillow. "So you're not on the rebound. I can't believe that someone hasn't knocked himself out to be involved with you." Her eyes were so open and so honest that he hated himself for a minute.

"I was involved. Very involved. I was engaged. Living in Atlanta, working for a magazine there. I...left."

"Why?"

"There were things I wanted from the relationship that I didn't think I could ever have." She hesitated and smiled. "I was engaged for a long time. We never managed to set a date for the wedding. I wanted children. Peter thought it was wrong to bring them into this world, that there might have been things wrong with him from the war...he just wasn't ready, I suppose. I don't know. I was there for him for too long."

"Did you love him?"

"Yes."

"Then what would happen if he changed his mind?"

"I don't know anymore. I already feel as if I've been gone for a very long time. Now you. Where are you from? I thought New York when you mentioned being friends with an actress. But you don't have a New York accent. Actually, it's not a Midwest twang or a Southern drawl, either. California?"

He caught her hands and kissed her fingers. "Don't ask questions, Amber. I told you, I'm from all over."

"English isn't your first language, is it?"

The question startled him. No one could question his English. It was perfect.

"Of course it is," he lied. "Amber, I've warned you. I have nothing real to give, and I won't answer questions."

Her lashes fell over her eyes. He had hurt her, and he was sorry. He'd started this, and he never should have. He couldn't let her get close; she was bright and intuitive, and it was dangerous to be with her.

It was just that when he was with her, he felt as if he had been healed.

"What *am* I allowed to talk about?" she asked quietly.

He rested on one elbow and smoothed the hair away from her face with an easy smile. "Paris. In the springtime, summer, winter or fall. The way the Capitol building looks at sunset, so white and glorious against the magenta sky.''

"So you do like D.C.?"

"I love it."

"And Virginia?"

"I love it, too. The mountains and the valleys. There really is no place more beautiful on this earth. Yes, wait, maybe there is."

"And where is that?"

"That beach yesterday. That beach where I held you. Where we first made love." Yes, he had made love to her. And he hadn't really made love in a long, long time.

Forgive me, Sonia, he thought. But he knew that she would have forgiven him long ago. He was the one who could not forgive, and it was he who could not give himself absolution.

Maybe, once he had waged war on the Death Squad, he could find peace.

"Oh!" she murmured suddenly, glancing at the dial of her gold watch. "We're late. Dinner started ten minutes ago." She rose and searched for the black lace panties. Adam found them and rose, moving toward her. She reached for them and slipped into them, then had trouble with the hooks on her bra.

"Let me help you," Adam said, but when he touched her, his fingers were suddenly trembling, and he knew it would be a mistake, that he would want to start everything all over again. "Never mind— I don't think that would be such a wonderful idea," he murmured. She smiled. He kissed her lips and turned away, drawing a dress shirt from his closet.

In minutes they were ready, checking out one another's appearances like guilty schoolchildren. Adam escorted Amber down the hallway and the stairs, but when they got near the dining room, he hesitated. "Do you want to go in alone?"

"Not unless you want me to."

He shook his head. "You do know that your father wouldn't want you seeing me?"

"Yes, I know. I wish you would tell me why."

"I can't."

She studied him gravely for a moment. "All right. I believe you. And no, I do not want to go in alone."

He grinned and took her arm.

When they reached the table, the men rose. Amber apologized for being late but gave no excuse. She needed none. Myra commented that it was a cruise, a vacation, and that they shouldn't be on a strict time-table. Senator Daldrin smiled, too, but he was study-ing them both, and Amber thought he looked worried.

The group spent some time in the casino that night. Ian loved to play blackjack, but he gambled on a low and careful scale, too much the politician to allow the opposition any opportunity to attack his life-style.

Michael Adams was a somewhat careless gambler, Amber thought. He played blackjack and roulette, and no emotion ever showed on his features, and he seemed to do well enough, winning more often than he lost.

While he was still engaged in a game, Amber slipped out on deck. She liked her spot in the shadows where she could stare at the water.

A few minutes later she realized that Senator Daldrin was outside again, too, staring at the darkness.

She looked around to see if she could see Michael. She couldn't, yet she sensed that he was near.

She heard movement and edged behind the lifeboat, into the shadows. Michael had suddenly appeared beside Ian Daldrin. She didn't think he had seen her, though. "Sir."

"Anything new?"

"No, not yet."

She was eavesdropping, she knew, but she stayed in the shadows anyway.

"What are you doing with Amber Larkspur?"

She couldn't see his brow arch, but she could feel it. He would be staring at Daldrin, not rudely, but with a cold gaze that suggested the question was none of his business.

"Sir, may I remind you that you insisted I look after her?"

"Yes, I did. But I didn't suggest . . ."

"What?"

"I don't know. You tell me."

"I'll tell you, sir. With all due respect, it's none of your business. It's between Amber and me."

Daldrin didn't speak for several long seconds. "She means a lot to me, and everything to Ted. I wouldn't want to see her hurt."

"I don't want to see anyone hurt."

"None of us does."

Amber started to shift her position and cracked her head against the lifeboat. Both men swung around. She walked toward them, wondering whether to let them know that she had heard them. She shouldn't have been eavesdropping. Neither of them really had a right to dictate her life. She smiled. She wasn't going to let them know. "Hello. It's beautiful out here, isn't it?"

"Yes, very beautiful," Ian Daldrin said.

"More people should enjoy the view. It seems to me that we're the only ones who are ever out here at night."

"Don't spoil a good thing," Daldrin said with a wink. "Would you like a nightcap, Amber? Michael?"

"Yes, I think that would be nice," she said after a moment's thought.

He led her inside, and they decided on the Star Lounge, high atop the ship. Michael Adams walked behind them up the stairs. They had to go out on deck again to take the last flight of stairs to the small lounge.

Daldrin was preceding Amber on the steps. She paused suddenly, aware that Michael was no longer with them. He was on the deck. One of the crewmen had stopped him.

Amber started down the steps. "Tomorrow night." She heard the words as if they were the tail end of a sentence. The dark man speaking with Michael had a heavy accent, but she didn't know what type of accent it was. The crewmen came from many nations.

"Definitely?" Michael said, his voice sharp and tense.

The man replied in a foreign language that Michael seemed to understand easily. He answered the man in kind, then turned.

He stopped, his foot on the first stair when he saw Amber. He stared at her, displeased and furious, though it seemed that he was trying to mask his emotions. "What are you doing there?"

"Waiting for you."

"Oh. Well, then, let's go on up, shall we?"

"Yes, I'm sure the senator's waiting for us."

When they reached the top of the stairs, Michael suddenly spun Amber around. "What did you hear?"

"Nothing."

"You're lying."

She tossed back her hair. "All right, I'm lying. What's tomorrow night?"

"A poker game. And you're not invited. And neither is anyone else in our party, do you understand?"

His fingers were wound tightly around her arm. "Michael, you're hurting me. I'm not going to tell anyone about your absurd little poker party. Let go. You'd think I was walking around with a national secret."

His fingers loosened. "I'm sorry. I just don't want anyone to know."

"Isn't that rather petty?"

"Amber, I don't want anyone to know."

Why had she ever thought she had found warmth in him? His eyes were ice, pure ice. His touch was as cold and brutal as steel.

She moved away from him. He was a dangerous lover. And yet she had chosen him, and she knew that she wasn't going to stay away. For the moment, though, she turned her back on him and swung open the door to the lounge.

Senator Daldrin had commandeered a table with a beautiful view of the night. In the distance they could see the lights from another cruise ship. "What kept you two?" Daldrin asked pleasantly.

"Oh, a cabin steward stopped me, sir. I'd lost a cufflink, he found it."

Amber glanced at Michael. He had spoken the lie easily, staring straight into Daldrin's eyes.

"Good. It's always nice when they know something we don't."

"Yes. That's a good steward. He knows what he's doing."

The senator signaled a waitress, and they ordered, a cognac for Daldrin, a white crème de menthe for Amber, a neat Scotch for Michael.

Daldrin leaned against the table, looking out at the night. "The moon will still be nearly full tomorrow night."

"Yes," Michael Adams replied. "The moon will still be full."

The senator nodded slightly. Something had passed between the two of them that had caused the senator to shudder slightly. For the life of her, Amber couldn't figure out what it was.

Their drinks arrived. The senator lifted his glass. "To beautiful ocean cruises, to freedom and the night, and to the moon, when it's full!"

Amber and Michael lifted their glasses. The senator looked morose, but Michael Adams betrayed no emotion, then or later, when he walked her to her cabin. Outside the door he took her hands. "Good night, Amber."

"Good night."

Then he muttered a soft oath and kissed the back of her hands, then her palms, before he pulled her into his arms and kissed her in the way that left her weak and breathless and wanting more of him every time.

Then he pulled away, touched her cheek gently and walked off down the hallway.

Montego Bay
June 15

Amber didn't see Michael Adams or the senator in the morning. She took off with Josie and Jim to wander around the quaint and busy streets of Montego Bay, and then to take a tour of Rose Hall, the beautiful old plantation where the White Witch had ruled in decadent splendor, beating and murdering her slaves while carrying on various affairs. The place was glorious, their guide lively and fun, and Amber enjoyed the morning, except that she kept wondering about Michael, where he might be and what he might be doing. There was no commitment between them, she reminded herself. None at all.

Yet when they had gone through the house, and she was standing outside in the garden, feeling the Jamaican sunshine on her cheeks, she was surprised to feel a curious sensation ripple along her spine. She spun around to find him looking at her from a distance of twenty feet or so.

She didn't speak, but waited for him to do so. He ambled toward her in cutoff jeans and a polo shirt and his dark glasses.

"I didn't know you were on the tour," she said.

"I wasn't, really. I've been out here."

"Senator Daldrin?"

"He's still in the house. Where are the Bainbridges?"

"Still inside."

He nodded.

"Are you watching me?" she asked him.

"At the moment, yes."

"That's not what I mean."

"The senator seems to be concerned about you."

"Has it all been his concern?"

"You know better than that."

Jim and Josie were coming out of the house. Josie smiled when she saw Michael. "We're going to a hotel for a drink. The one with the pool lagoon. Would you like to come?"

Amber wished she could see his eyes. He shook his head, and she thought there was real regret in his voice. "Sorry. I'm waiting for the senator."

"Oh, well, feel free to join us later," Josie said.

Michael nodded. He watched Amber as she followed the pair out to the small car they had rented.

To Amber's surprise, the senator, Michael Adams and several other members of the party did join them later. The bar was in the center of the lagoon, and they had all stripped down to bathing suits to swim over. Then Amber had crawled up on a huge float and drifted beneath the sun. She half closed her eyes and saw the brilliance of the burning orb in the sky, then let her lashes fall completely. When she opened her eyes seconds later, she saw Michael, seated by the pool, sipping something from a pineapple and staring at her. She made no move toward him. Nor did he come near her. He was staying away, she knew, because he wanted it to be her move. Daldrin didn't want them together. Michael wouldn't deny a relationship, but if she wanted to, he would give her the opportunity.

She wasn't sure just what she wanted anymore.

They returned to the ship soon after, since they were due to leave port before dark and head for the Mexican coast. Amber showered and changed quickly, choosing white that night. Her gown was intricately beaded at the bodice but had a flowing skirt that complimented her every movement. When Myra came in to change, Amber chatted for a moment about her day, then left the cabin.

Her heart was beating with a thunderous flutter, and she didn't want to admit it. She didn't want to think about what she was doing. But she headed along the hall to Michael's cabin. When she got to the door she lifted her hand, and a wealth of color flooded her face before she knocked. She was going to his cabin to make love with him, and she couldn't believe how bold she was being.

The door opened. He had showered, too. He was in briefs, with a hint of shaving cream still on his cheeks. His expression seemed grave, regretful again.

And then he pulled her into the cabin. She felt the warmth of his arms enveloping her, and any sense of shame fled quickly.

He disrobed her very carefully that night, then made love to her more intensely, more passionately, than ever before. When they lay entwined together after it was over, he continued to touch her as their bodies cooled slowly in the sea air. Then he swept her into his arms again, holding her tightly. "My God, I'm going to miss you," he whispered.

A deep chill touched her heart. He had always said that he had nothing to give her. And she had entered their relationship asking for nothing; she still didn't know what she wanted out of life. A month ago she had wanted Peter to cry out his devotion, to swear that he would set a date, would speak seriously about children. But lying here, she couldn't imagine that she wouldn't experience Michael Adams again, with his energy and his vibrance and his passion. She moistened her lips as his head bent low over her breast, as his tongue touched and teased her flesh, tasting her curiously, tenderly.

She had no hold on him. But neither was the cruise anywhere near over.

She wove her fingers through the tawny wealth of his hair. She was about to speak when he leaned over her and spoke bitterly himself. "Damn you, Amber. Damn you. This never should have happened."

He rose. She was left, bereft and cold and confused, and she suddenly felt very naked. She leaped up, reached for her clothing and dressed quickly, her fingers trembling. He was still knotting his tie when she slipped on her second shoe and headed for the door.

"Amber!"

"What?"

She was reaching for the doorknob and when he slammed the door shut, her temper soared. "Just let—"

His mouth closed over hers. His kiss was hot and passionate and demanding, then achingly sweet, and it seemed to steal all her strength. Then his lips rose just slightly, and she felt his tempest again. His whisper was harsh, yet still his hold upon her was tender. "Damn you, damn you for making me want you."

Suddenly he wasn't holding her anymore. She turned and fled from the room, hurrying to dinner.

It was a stilted meal. The senator was as tense as Michael. The others drifted away from the table early, until only Michael, the senator and Amber remained. "What are you doing tonight?" the senator asked her.

She arched a brow. "Nothing special. I'll probably walk on deck and maybe visit one of the lounges."

"Visit the lounge." Michael's hand was on hers, and he issued the words as an order.

She stared at his bronzed hand. What was it that he was doing tonight? Ah, yes, that all-important poker game. She smiled. "Please don't worry about me. I am well able to find my own entertainment."

"Yes, I know. But you shouldn't be wandering alone on deck at night. Visit the lounge. Go to bed early."

Daldrin cleared his throat. "Amber is a grown woman, you know." Those words sounded like a warning, too. She was losing her mind. She didn't know if the two men liked or hated one another, or why they were being so confusing, so enigmatic. She stood. She didn't know what Michael's problem was this evening, but he had left her feeling more lost and confused than ever. More than anything, she wanted to be alone on deck. She wanted to hear the ocean and see the darkness and stand and let the breeze soothe her.

"I'll see the movie tonight, I think. Thank you, and excuse me."

She smiled sweetly and walked away. Michael was on his feet, too. She thought for a moment that he was going to follow her, but he didn't. Instead he spoke to the senator, then left the dining room by the port door.

Amber hurried outside. The night was beautiful. The darkness, the whisper of the breeze, all closed around her.

Damn you, Michael! she thought.

Chapter 7

The Alexandria, *International Waters*
June 15, 12:45 a.m.

He was running late. What a fool he was. He should have left things alone; he shouldn't have been so intense; he shouldn't have shouted out orders. There were a million other places on the ship where she might be. There was no reason to worry that Amber might run right into things.

In his cabin, he glanced at his watch. He had learned this morning that the boat would come between twelve-thirty and one o'clock. One nice thing about the senator being in on the plan was that he hadn't needed to play any games. He'd told the man the time and the place, and that had been that. But now he had to plunge into the act, and his concentration was off. It shouldn't be, but it was—and all because of her.

He would miss her....

Revenge was at hand. He had waited a long, long time to know for certain, and now he did. And there just happened to be something noble that could be achieved, too—freedom for others. For the four military advisers, the two diplomats and the two bankers. And Daldrin and himself. He hoped that Daldrin would come out all right. The man had courage. Very few men would willingly step into the power of the Death Squad.

Adam quickly discarded his dress suit, then zipped up black jeans and pulled a black turtleneck over his head. He tied on black sneakers and flipped up his mattress to find his weapons, sliding his pistol into his waistband and his knife into the sheath at his calf. He took a look around the room, then abandoned it. He wanted to be on deck the moment the assailants arrived just in case something went wrong. He didn't want to take any chances with innocent lives.

He went up to the Bahamas Deck. He could hear loud salsa music pouring out from the lounge as he hurried to the door opening to the forward lifeboat area. He glanced at his watch. It was time.

The second he opened the door, he heard the screams.

Damn! It had all gone to hell, straight to hell. Worse than that.

Amber.

Amber was on the floorboards, and one of Abdul's cutthroats was straddled over her, his knife about to connect with her jugular. Adam raced forward in a blind fury, wrenching the man up and around.

He had forgotten. For a moment he had actually forgotten his role. He had heard her scream, had seen her lying there, had seen the flash of the blade. Nothing else had mattered then, not even revenge. Not even the eight men on the island. Nothing.

The danger was over. He left Amber where she lay and began to rail against her attacker in swift and furious Spanish. He reminded the man that he was in control, that the orders had been no violence on the ship, no bloodshed.

"Michael!" she whispered.

Run! he wanted to shout to her. Run away quickly. I'll stop them....

"Michael...thank God!" she said. Her eyes were wide, her hair wild, everything about her feminine and trusting. And Abdul's men were laughing and snickering as she pitched herself into his arms.

Damn her. Damn her a thousand times over. She shouldn't have been on deck. He shouldn't feel for her the things that he did, and she shouldn't trust him. He shouldn't be relishing her warmth against him while he desperately wondered how to save her life. And her eyes shouldn't be on him, so beautiful, but wide with dawning horror and reproach and fury.

"No, Amber," he said softly. "No, I'm sorry. I'm not here to help you."

"You bastard."

Her hatred hurt. The depth of his pain was startling, like the twist of a knife. He lowered his face and whispered softly to her, "Damn you, Amber, you should have run, you little fool!"

She wrenched away from him, and this time she did start to run. But he couldn't allow her to get away. The others would kill her, given half a chance. He caught her by the hair and jerked her into his arms. He glared at her warningly, his fingers tightening in her hair.

"She has to be killed," one of the men began in Spanish.

"No!" His grip grew ever tighter. He needed to hold her still and keep her silent.

"Let me go!" she shrieked.

He clapped a hand down hard over her mouth. "Shut up, Miss Larkspur," he whispered to her. "Shut up. *Now*. I'm doing my best to save your miserable little interfering life!" His touch was brutal, his words harsh. They had to be. The fellow he had decked for nearly killing her was up and at the railing and looking down. The men who had already taken the senator must surely be wondering what the hell was going on. He switched languages, speaking in Arabic to demonstrate his authority. "Signal that we're coming down, that we're bringing an extra hostage."

He dared not show his relief when the man obeyed him. He couldn't leave Amber—they wouldn't allow that. He had to take her; there was no other choice. Then he had to hope and pray that he could still pull this whole damn thing off.

If only she had listened to him! If only she hadn't been on deck.

But she had been. And now she was in his arms, and he was going to have to keep her there if he was going to keep her alive. He whispered harshly to Amber. "This is my party, Miss Larkspur. You weren't invited, but you're here." He slowly eased his hold on her mouth.

She started to scream again. Furious, desperate, he swore. "Damn you!" He clamped his hand tightly over her mouth again. "Stop it!" he hissed. If she screamed again, someone might well stab her, whether he was holding her or not. "Amber, I'll give you one warning—"

She bit him.

He released her and slammed his fist against her jaw.

She slumped into his arms, and he looked at the men. "What the hell are you staring at?" he demanded sharply, reverting to Spanish again. "Let's get going." He gestured to the strong rope dangling from the rail.

The men crawled down the rope easily, silently. Adam followed with less grace, balancing Amber's weight. When he fell the last few feet to the small motor launch, he tried to break her fall with his body. The small boat pitched and swayed as Adam crawled along the floor to sit on the far aft seat, staring straight ahead. Two of the men flanked Daldrin, who sat in silence between them. The one who had tried to kill Amber stared at Adam, fury in his eyes, but Adam ignored him. A third man was behind him, and the last was gunning the engine, heading into the darkness of the night.

Twenty minutes later, in the midst of an inky eternity, they came upon a cabin cruiser. It was small compared with the *Alexandria*, but big and beautiful compared with others of its classification. It was a good sixty-five feet long, Adam was certain.

The launch pulled up alongside the cruiser, where Ali Abdul, still in his desert robes despite the humidity of the tropics, waited on deck as the ladder was lowered.

"What's this?" he demanded when he saw Adam.

"A woman. She was on deck."

"You should have thrown her over the rail," someone advised sharply. It was Khazar, coming from behind his father. He stared down dispassionately at Adam's feminine burden.

"I told them no bloodshed on the ship," Ali said. His voice was low, but it was still the voice of command.

"If you intend to hurt that woman," Daldrin said, speaking at last, "you may as well kill me here and now. I'll be no bargaining pawn for you if she is harmed."

"We'll discuss it—" Khazar began.

"There will be no discussion," Adam said flatly. He threw Amber over his shoulder and swung aboard the cabin cruiser. "She's mine. I will look after her, and I will see to her behavior."

"Father," Khazar began angrily, "since when do American riffraff and politicians tell you what to do?"

"I have proven myself," Adam said simply. "I am here. Daldrin is here, as you wished. Without me, you never would have gotten past the American security."

"I tell you, if she's hurt—" Daldrin began.

"Shut him up!" Khazar ordered.

Still balancing Amber's unconscious weight, Adam reached down and grasped the senator's hand. "Come on up, old man," he said.

"Take him to the forward cabin. Lock him in and leave a guard," Ali ordered. He was instantly obeyed. Then he turned to stare at Adam. "You take orders from me. Leave her in the galley, for now. I will hear more."

There was a door to a large cabin behind the mainmast and wheel. Adam strode through it, carrying Amber down a small flight of steps and over to a sofa against the wall. There was no sign that he had struck her, as yet. She seemed asleep, beautiful, peaceful. He prayed that he could maintain his authority. He was afraid of what they would do to her if he didn't.

He paused, unable to forget the sense of betrayal he had seen in her eyes.

"Adam. Come topside and speak to me."

Ali was leaning through the doorway. Adam nodded and left Amber, hurrying up the steps.

Ali was seated with men hovering around him: the four in the wet suits who had been with Adam on the deck of the *Alexandria*; two additional swarthy men, both a little older than the others. "Khazar is with our guest, the senator," Ali told Adam. "Raphael, Juan, Jose and Jaime are with our Central American faction, as you know. This is Mohammed beside me, and over here, Aladin. My very good friends for many long years. Now, tell me, what is the woman doing here?"

"And why is she yours?" the one named Juan demanded.

"I answer to Ali Abdul and no other man," Adam said.

Ali watched him, then nodded. "Yes, that is so. You answer to me alone."

"She is my mistress," he said.

"You were not permitted to bring a mistress."

"I did not intend to do so. We became lovers when I infiltrated the senator's office. I had arranged for her to be elsewhere, but she wandered out on deck. She entered into this by accident. But she is mine, and I will keep her silent and well behaved."

Ali waited a long time before he replied. "Tomorrow we come to the island. You will see that there is no trouble. If there is, she dies."

"I will see that she understands."

"Juan, see if the woman has awakened. If she has, bring her to me."

Juan did as he was told. Ali watched Adam. "You will explain to the Americans that the Fourth of July will bring them great tragedy if they do not meet my demands."

"Yes, I understand. How will I communicate with them?"

"I will send you to Mexico. You will communicate there."

Adam turned as he realized that Amber had been brought to the canopied helm area. She was shoeless, her elegant scarf was gone, and her chin was very high despite the terror and fury in her eyes. From her shoulders to her toes, she was proud and beautiful, every inch a desirable woman. He knew that Juan felt it, too, and he told Ali softly, "Make him understand that the woman is mine. He may not touch her."

Juan exploded in fury. "Are we not brothers? Do we not share? She was not welcome, but she is here. She will be nothing but trouble."

"She is my concern." Adam insisted. "Mine."

An argument broke out, and Juan kept repeating that he, too, had a right to the woman. The older men, Ali's companions, were impatient, saying that Adam had his rights.

Then Amber spoke, silencing them all. "What the hell is going on?" she exploded. "None of you has any rights where I'm concerned. You're criminals! You let me go—and the senator—this instant or I swear I shall—"

"Ali, let me handle her," Adam said in Arabic. He needed to get her alone, even though he couldn't explain to her who he was yet. She was in a panic, and she might easily betray him or she might not believe him. Then they'd all be dead. If she didn't stop, the only way to handle things would be to hurt her.

"Where is the senator?" Amber demanded.

"Shut up!" Adam ordered.

She didn't shut up. "They'll hang you, Adams. They'll get you, you bastard, one way or the other. Maybe they'll shoot you for treason. It's—" He didn't want to hear any more of her words.

"Shut up, Amber," he warned her again.

"The hell I will—"

He reached her before she could move and slapped her hard across the cheek. The stunned pain that entered her eyes seemed to reach into his soul, but he didn't dare falter. She had to be cowed.

She wasn't. She struck him back with a blow that rang in his ears.

Laughter rose. Laughter. Juan roared out that Adam's *puta* wore the pants. She heard the word, and she understood it. Eyes wide, she protested, "No! I'm nothing to this man! Listen to me—"

"Shut up!" Adam thundered. He didn't dare let her go on. He clamped one hand over her mouth, grabbed her with the other and tossed her over his shoulder. He had to regain the men's respect. He faced Ali. "There's a private cabin for me?"

Ali nodded. Amber fought wildly as Adam hurried down the stairs with her, passing through the galley and salon before he pushed open a door to reveal a cabin with a narrow bunk. He tossed her down on it, but she rose, still fighting.

He pushed her backward and stripped off his shirt. If she wanted a fight, she was going to get one. And she was going to lose.

She had gone silent, watching him strip off his shirt. In the pale light her hair spilled over her shoulders, and he ached to possess her. He hardened himself against her.

"Let me go, you son of a bitch!" she demanded.

He unbuckled his belt and pulled it from his belt loops, wrapping the end around his hand and locking his jaw as she started to scream. He let loose with the belt, striking the bunk with vehemence. She stared at him.

"Dear God . . ." she gasped.

He took a step toward the bed and wrenched her against him. "Scream again," he ordered curtly.

"What?"

"Scream again."

"Michael, I don't—"

"You idiot, I said *scream*!"

She was still staring at him, tense and trembling and beautiful, but not uttering a sound. He gritted his teeth still more tightly, and then he knew. He knew what would make her scream.

He released her shoulders and caught hold of her bodice, wrenching it apart. She fought him, letting out a scream that brought a grim smile to his lips.

"Good scream," he said, splitting the gown to her navel. She fell back on the bunk, trying to hold her clothing and her dignity together. He sat down and removed his sneakers.

"I'll kill you myself!" she swore.

He stripped off his jeans, leaving his knife hidden under the pants. He set his gun on the bureau. If they were disturbed in the night, he wanted it to be obvious that they'd been together.

She was staring at him with horror and hatred, and he suddenly realized what he was doing. They'd been together so intimately that it hadn't seemed to matter, but now he saw that it did. It mattered to her. Suddenly the hatred in her eyes disturbed him. She might have realized that he was trying to keep her alive; she might have known enough about him not to believe in the evil that she saw.

"No..." she whispered.

"Amber, my love," he mocked her, "there's nothing new here."

She flew at him like a wildcat, and he warned her to stop. When she didn't, he told her to give herself a chance. But in the end he had to subdue her, his naked form atop her.

Finally a single word left her lips. A plea. "Don't..."

"Listen to me. And listen good. I am trying to keep you alive."

She was never, never going to believe him. He saw it in her eyes. Damn her. He levered himself away from her, running his fingers through his hair. What she felt didn't matter, he reminded himself hollowly. He hadn't loved her, hadn't told her that he loved her; he had just wanted her. And he had admired her. He still admired her. But he didn't love her; he was still in love with Sonia. Amber could think what she wanted.

As long as she came to heel. No matter how cold or cruel he had to be, he had to make her come to heel.

He heard her inhale, and he turned around. She was only half-clad, her hair streaming around her shoulders, those beautiful, reproachful eyes of hers condemning him straight to hell. Well, that might well be his destination.

The gown was in tatters. It wasn't any good anymore. And if they were visited in the night . . .

"Take that off," he told her.

"No, Michael. No, I—"

She wouldn't admit defeat. And he was exhausted, his nerves on edge. He grabbed a handful of her hair and pulled her close. He felt the silken strands against his fingers, and his fury increased all the more. In the midst of all this tempest, he wanted her still, wanted her more than ever, wanted her moving against him, her breath on his naked flesh, her hips fluid, her hair softly brushing his chest. But it was over. It would never happen again.

Then she spat at him.

He waited. He waited for the fury and the hunger and the bitterness to subside. She vowed to kill him again, and he ignored her. Then she tried to grab the gun, and he could no longer ignore her. Calmly, forcefully, coldly, with grim determination, he stripped away her clothing and tossed it heedlessly to the floor. When she lay completely naked, he left her alone at last and walked to the cabin door, where he listened carefully.

What had they heard topside? It was important that they think he had subdued her and punished her for her behavior. Well, they should believe that now, he thought wearily.

She was crying. Crying at last. He wanted to dig a hole in the ocean floor and crawl into it.

Amber Larkspur wasn't the only one at risk here. There were eight men depending on him on the island, and Senator Daldrin.

And still, to know that she was flinching from him...

He tightened his hands into fists. It should have been over. She should have been a memory.

But she wasn't. She was lying in the bunk where he would spend the night—without touching her. "Get under the blanket and move over," he told her. "Quickly."

She protested, and wearily, he repeated his order, then gestured for silence.

He lay down and listened again. They had finished talking about him and Amber. They were musing about what action the President of the United States would take when he was confronted with their new threats and demands.

Amber was inching closer and closer to the wall. Should he be in the cabin with her like this, he wondered, when there was a loaded gun at hand?

He turned to her, fierce, furious. "One warning, Miss Larkspur. Don't play me for a fool. You're supposed to be an intelligent woman. Prove it. Whatever I say, do. Whatever game I play, you play along. Understand?"

"They'll hang you!" she vowed. "They'll hang you, or they'll shoot you—"

He closed his hand over her mouth. So much for peace between them. He could never relax his guard. He was fighting the enemy, and he was fighting his own side, too. For the moment, it was the only way.

He smiled grimly at her. "Then perhaps I should make it worth my while." He cast his leg intimately over hers. He would never take her by force, but she wouldn't know that.

She went stiff and silent. Silent at last.

He wanted to touch her, to soothe her. He wanted to pull her into his arms and reassure her. Most of all, he just wanted to hold her, to see the hatred fade from her eyes. But he couldn't do any of those things. "I am trying to help you," he told her. "Do you understand?"

"Obviously," she said scathingly.

"I'm sorry. I'm sorry you got involved."

"You're a traitor, you bastard!"

His hand wrapped convulsively around hers. If he was caught, if he was killed on the island, the whole world would believe that what she said was true. His muscles tightened, and he felt his anger growing, despite his resolve. "What I am doesn't matter, Amber. Not if you want to survive this."

Again, she lay silent. He swallowed his anger. If she just weren't so damn brave, if she didn't fight him so fiercely...

Then a slight sob escaped her. The sound stabbed his heart and tore through his insides. He couldn't help himself. He had held her; he had touched her. He had loved her.

He turned to her, stroking her cheek. "It will be all right. I promise, it will be all right."

She shoved his hand away. "Fine. So you say. Just—just don't touch me."

She didn't want his touch. Not anymore. She couldn't bear his hands upon her. It was natural for her to feel that way. For the moment, it was even necessary.

"I'll do my best...Miss Larkspur," he promised her coldly.

But he *was* touching her, or nearly so. He was beside her, their naked bodies nearly meeting. He had known her so very well, the sound of her voice, every nuance of her form, the sweet, subtle scent of her....

He turned his back on her, but he could still feel her, still see her. He could see her beautiful aquamarine eyes, see her face when he touched her, the fall of her hair.

He could turn his back on her, but she was still there.

He could feel her warmth, and he could breathe her perfume. He knew that he could turn over again and she would be there.

It was going to be a very long night.

And the days that stretched ahead would be even longer.

Chapter 8

June 16

The explosive sound of the door bursting open brought Amber instantly from the deep sleep she had finally fallen into. Panicked, she jerked up, and even as she did so, Michael's arms came around her, pulling the blanket over her naked shoulders and breasts and bearing her back to the bed. She opened her mouth to scream in protest, but she fell silent when she saw the tall, dark man in the doorway.

Michael was swearing at him in Arabic.

The man was as distinctive as Michael in appearance. His eyes were as dark as the night, but alive with fire and fury. His complexion was olive, his facial structure striking, and yet there was such cruelty in the curve of his mouth and in his eyes that she found herself shivering in his presence. She didn't think he had been topside when she had been dragged up last night. She didn't think she would have forgotten him.

And there seemed to be open warfare between him and Michael. One snapped out something; the other replied. She felt the tension and fury and heat in Michael's body. If she wasn't there—or if there weren't others aboard the boat, perhaps—she was certain they would have leaped at one another like a pair of competing tigers.

And if they did . . .

Dear God, she didn't want to fall into that man's hands. From the way he gestured at her, she knew she was the cause of their current argument.

And God help her, as much as she despised Michael for what he had done, for what he was, she didn't want to fall to his enemy.

Dark, burning eyes fell on her. Then the door slammed, and the silence that ensued was almost painful.

Michael's arms were still around her, covering her with the blanket. She flinched away from him as far as she could, her body against the paneling.

Michael lay flat, pressing his temples between his hands. "Oh, God," he groaned. "So that's the way it's going to be." He didn't glance her way; he just stared at the ceiling and sighed, and he seemed so weary that a curious quiver touched her heart. He was a traitor, a monster, she reminded herself. And she would fight him until she died.

He spoke harshly to her then. "Amber, you're playing with fire here. I'm warning you, I'm threat-

ening you, I'm doing everything in my power to make
you understand. Listen to me, pay attention to me—
it's your only chance.''

She didn't move. She wanted to burst into tears and
claw at him, but she didn't move. She swallowed hard.
''Who was that?'' she demanded.

''Khazar Abdul. Ali Abdul's son.''

She felt a quaking inside again. Ali Abdul was well-
known; the newspapers had written about him a dozen
times.

They had also written articles on his son. Khazar
was crazy, in her opinion. He had no respect for life.
He would kill without blinking an eye; he would send
his own men into suicidal situations and assure himself that he had given them their entrance into heaven.

Michael rose on one elbow and faced her. In the
close confines of the bunk she could feel the warmth
emanating from his body. ''I told him that he had no
right to interrupt my privacy. His argument is that I
have no right to privacy. Unless you want to get to
know Khazar and his Latin friends very, very well, you
need to lie low, Miss Larkspur, and stay behind me
every second. Is that clear?''

She didn't reply; she couldn't. Words caught in her
throat, a silent scream close behind. She had been
falling in love with him despite all his warnings, and
now she could not believe, could not accept, what he
was.

He didn't wait for an answer. He swung his feet over
the side of the bed and reached for his clothing. He
dressed, ignoring her, then turned to her. ''Get some-

thing on. And don't make a move. Unless one of them comes for you. Then you can scream like hell."

"I can't get dressed," she snapped out. "You destroyed my gown last night."

"Oh, yes. Then I'd hug that blanket tight for the time being if I were you."

He exited the cabin. She laid her head down and felt the dampness of tears as they trickled down her cheeks. They were still at sea, she realized after a moment. She could feel the movement of the boat.

After several moments she roused herself and realized that she could don her underwear, if nothing else. She did so, then pulled the blanket around her shoulders again. Desperately she looked around the cabin for something that resembled a weapon, should she need one, but she couldn't find anything that might help her. Michael had very carefully picked up his gun, and there was nothing else around.

Just as she sat down on the bunk, the door swung open. She jerked back, afraid of who it might be, then despised herself because she breathed a sigh of relief when she saw that it was Michael. He was as bad as the rest of them, she reminded herself, no matter how hard it was to accept that fact.

He had a bundle in his arms, and tossed it toward the bed. "It's a skirt and blouse." She must have stared distastefully at the wrapped up garments, because he continued. "They're clean. They've never been touched. Jaime bought them for his sister last week in Mexico. Be grateful."

"Be grateful that you kidnapped me and tore my own clothes off me?"

His teeth locked, and his eyes turned as cold as ice. "Be grateful that you're not running around naked, that you didn't spend the night with Khazar Abdul." He started to turn. She must have gone a little mad, or perhaps something snapped inside her. She cried out and lunged at him with new fury, trying desperately to hurt him.

She couldn't. He quickly caught her wrists and dragged them beneath her back, and she was left staring at him, crushed against him. His eyes burned into hers, and his voice fell softly. "If you don't want to be touched, Miss Larkspur, don't throw yourself against me wearing scanty white lace."

Color flooded her cheeks. "You are scum," she told him.

He released her, shoving her toward the bunk, and left the cabin.

Amber quickly picked up the clothes he had given her: a white cotton blouse with pretty embroidery and a full blue skirt with the same embroidery along the hem.

It seemed ironic to her that a terrorist would have a sister and that, during his free time, he would shop for her.

The garments were new and clean, and she was glad to put them on, even if her fingers were trembling as she did so. When she was dressed she sat at the foot of the bed with her hands folded and tried to still the beating of her heart.

No one came. Exhausted, she stretched out on the bunk and closed her eyes. To her amazement, she slept. When she awoke, she was still alone. She stared at the wood-paneled ceiling of the small cabin, then looked toward the cruiser's curtained windows, sat up and pulled aside one of the small drapes to look out.

They were still on the water, but she thought that they might just have pulled away from some port, because there was a large land mass in the distance, and there were a number of pleasure boats near them, beautiful sailboats and smaller craft.

She wondered if she could break a window and scream. But no one would hear her, she knew.

Frustrated, she sat again on the bed. She could hear men talking topside, but she couldn't make out a single word they were saying.

She heard the soft tread of footsteps beyond the door and quickly tensed. Was it Michael, or was it someone else? Did it matter?

She shivered, wondering how the man could have turned out to be such a traitor. It felt as if her very heart had gone cold with the shock of it. Maybe he hadn't done it on purpose, but he had brought her into the hands of the Death Squad. She might very well die.

The door opened. This time it wasn't Michael; it was one of the dark-haired men from the night before. He carried a tray covered with a cloth napkin. The man watched her and flashed a lascivious, white-toothed smile, as he put the tray on the bed. "You eat."

She didn't make a move. He touched her sleeve, and she jumped back. "Pretty, yes?"

She still didn't reply, and he shrugged. "I see you later."

Then he, too, was gone.

There seemed to be a tight knot in Amber's stomach, but she pulled the napkin off the tray anyway. She should eat, she knew. If she was ever to have a chance of escape, she would need strength.

There was a cup of steaming coffee there, with bread and butter and something that looked like a *palomillo* steak, a thin Latin steak, and plantains. She touched the napkin that had lain over the food. It was white and spotless. She looked around the cabin. It, too, was very clean.

Ali Abdul was apparently a fastidious man.

She sipped the coffee, then cut the thin steak and bit into it. It was very good. She found that she could eat. In fact, she consumed everything on the plate.

Senator Daldrin was still aboard somewhere. She hoped that he had been fed, as well. Maybe, if she could get to him, she could find more courage. They could escape together.

When she finished her food, she stood. She hadn't thought to try the door to the cabin. She did so, and found it unlocked. She stepped outside into the hallway. There was one man in the galley, at the sink. She looked in the opposite direction. There were other doors leading to other cabins. She kept an eye on the man in the galley and started checking out the other doors. She came upon an empty cabin, then another.

It occurred to her that there was another stretch of cabins on the aft side of the helm. With a sinking heart she realized that Senator Daldrin was probably there.

She threw open a fourth door. On a bunk lay some kind of automatic weapon. She hesitated, then hurried toward it.

"No, *chica*!" a voice called out. She spun. It was the man who had been in the galley, the man who had brought her the food. She lunged for the gun. Too late. He was on top of her, his weight pushing her down on the gun. She shoved against him, and to keep her from grabbing the weapon, he had to let her go.

She leaped up, tore down the hall and up the flight of steps leading to the deck.

They were there. They were all there. One man at the helm, the others seated in deck chairs or lined up along the rail. They were casually dressed in jeans and shorts, T-shirts and casual cotton knits.

Even Ali Abdul was dressed in loose shorts and a cotton shirt, his head covered but his burnoose gone. He stared at her.

Michael stood at the prow, his feet wide apart, balancing against the waves.

She looked from him to Ali, then to Khazar. The man from below was calling out a warning.

There was nowhere to go. Michael was spinning around to look at her when the Hispanic man appeared, the automatic rifle in his hands.

Amber made a mad dash for a space at the railing and dove into the sea. She sank into the cool, salty water, then kicked hard and reached the surface. There was land to the west, she knew. How far away was it? Did she have a prayer of making it? She didn't dare look back. They were in a motor cruiser. They could follow her; they could track her down and shoot her, just like some fishermen shoot sharks.

She started to swim, but the skirt weighed her down, tangling between her legs. She paused, treading water, trying to strip off the skirt.

A scream escaped her. A man was swimming toward her, hard. Michael. She turned and started to swim desperately again, but he caught her by the hair, wrenching her toward him. She sputtered and choked as water filled her mouth. He ignored her, carelessly stroking toward the boat. He moved powerfully, and no matter how she tried to twist from his painful hold, she was dragged cleanly through the water, irrevocably closer to the boat.

When they reached the cruiser, hands reached down to pull her up, then to assist Michael. She fell, defeated, into a wet pool on the deck. Michael stood over her. She could see his bare feet and calves and the water that dripped along them. "Don't ever try that again!" he ordered her sharply.

Her head was down. Someone approached them. She heard a voice speak in lightly accented English. Ali Abdul.

"It doesn't matter now. We have come to the Island of the Damned."

Amber looked up. They were indeed approaching an island. It seemed to be just off the mainland, small, yet its appearance could be deceptive. High mountains rose upon it, green and blue. It had apparently been formed by volcanic activity, and its appearance was similar to Jamaica.

The Island of the Damned. That was what Ali had called it.

And she was sure that that was what it would be for her. She had been brought to this secret place, and she was sure they would never let her leave it alive.

Everyone was silent as the boat slowed. They came closer and closer to the island, then slipped into a small channel between two tall walls of rock. Coral reefs were all around them. Amber could see the shoals beneath them. Only a seaman who knew the area well could possibly navigate here.

At long last they came to a cove with several docks, and the boat was maneuvered into a berth. There were other craft there, sailboats, motorboats, all different sizes and types. There were men on the docks, hosing down boats, cleaning fish. For a moment Amber felt her heart soar—there were other people on this island. Regular citizens. There might be hope.

But then one of the men saluted Ali as he stepped ashore with an agility rare for a man his age. Amber's heart sank to the pit of her stomach.

Michael's fingers tugged at her again. "Come on, Amber, we're here. The Island of the Damned."

She struggled to her feet, and he pushed her toward the rail. He leaped onto the dock ahead of her, then reached and swung her down. Her wet shirt dripped onto the dock, then Michael pointed ahead of them. "Our home," he said.

She looked in the direction he pointed, and chills seized her.

Ali's place was a fortress, built into the mountain, carved from the rock. It stood there, part of the landscape, barely discernible until you looked for it.

Michael shoved her forward. "There's a car waiting," he told her.

And there was. Ali Abdul awaited them in a Jeep. Michael pushed Amber along the dock until they reached the dirt road, where she climbed into the vehicle at his prodding.

Khazar sat beside her, pinning her between himself and Michael.

She looked straight ahead, and the Jeep roared to life. It took them down a long path to a door made of steel. Ali turned and looked at her. "Rock Fortress. It was built hundreds of years ago by the Spanish conquistadores. They brought the natives they could not subdue here, along with captured pirates and Englishmen, and they kept them in dungeons, or hanged them from the rocks when they tired of them." He smiled. "It became a training ground for revolutionaries. We are close to the countries who are often . . . not in accord with the United States. Now it is ours. Its history is fascinating. You must take time to hear about it."

Amber didn't answer him. Strands of wet hair lay plastered against her face, but she didn't bother to move them.

When the Jeep came to a stop Michael dragged her out on his side. The four of them started toward the steel door, which opened soundlessly. They entered a large room, where Michael spoke to Abdul in Arabic. The man replied, and then Michael led her down a long hallway to the right, stopping in front of a door at the far end. He opened it and thrust her inside.

She found herself in a simple bedroom, with a bed against one wall and a dresser against another. There was also a lock on the door.

Michael moved past her to throw open a second door. "The bathroom," he told her briefly. She was looking longingly at the door through which they had come. "Don't even think about it," he told her, then strode to it himself and walked out. She heard a key twist in the lock, and she raced toward the door, jerking on the knob. The door was solidly locked.

There wasn't even a window in the room.

She hurried into the bathroom. There was an old-fashioned tub, a sink and a toilet. But no window. Panic filled her. She had never felt so closed in. She hurried to the bedroom and slammed against the door. It didn't budge. She bit her lip and sank to the floor in despair.

It seemed like hours later when she heard the key in the door. She leaped up and backed away from it. The backs of her knees brushed the bed, and she sat down abruptly. The door opened.

Khazar had come with a tray of food. He walked into the room, letting the door fall shut but not locking it. He walked over to the dresser, staring at Amber, who watched him warily, afraid of the look in his eyes. He set down the tray, turned and looked at her, adjusting the band of his watch. For the longest time he stared at her. Then he started walking toward her. "You're wet. You must be cold and uncomfortable. We will find some things for you to wear."

Amber stood up as he neared her. Screaming, she lunged for the door, but he caught her and flung her back. He stood still for a moment, then pulled something from his pocket. Amber stared in horror as she realized it was a switchblade.

The door burst open. Michael stood there, looking first at Khazar, then at Amber. "What the hell's going on?" he demanded in English.

"Nothing is going on," Khazar said. He smiled at Amber. "I was going to cut her apple for her."

He turned and brushed past Michael, who stood there for several long moments, staring after Khazar. Finally he came into the room, closing the door and carefully locking it from the inside. He looked at Amber. "Did he hurt you?"

She shook her head.

He wanted to say more, she thought, but he didn't. He pulled off his sneakers and headed for the bathroom. A moment later Amber heard the shower.

She hesitated, thinking. She didn't want to meet up with Khazar again, and she *did* want to escape. Michael usually had a gun on him. But if he was in the shower, then for once his gun wasn't with him.

She silently opened the door to the bathroom, where a plastic curtain had been drawn around the old-fashioned tub.

Michael's clothing lay on the floor. His cutoffs were still damp from his dip in the ocean hours before; so were her own things. Damp and salty and stiff. She silently lifted the shorts. He must have a gun somewhere. Unless he had dived in with it and lost it. No, he wouldn't have done that.

She lifted his shirt. The gun was there, beneath it.

Wet hands fell on her shoulders. She screamed as she was lifted and set beneath the steady spray of the water. As he whirled her around to face him, the shower thundered over her face, her clothing. He held her close and spoke swiftly. "Amber, I will get you out of here—*if* you give me half a chance."

The water was hot, but she was shivering. There was something so fierce and passionate about his words. There was so much tension in him as he drew her to him. "But you've got to stop. I'm doing my best to keep you away from Khazar and the others, and you're making it almost impossible." He spoke softly, against the cacophony of the water, and he had looked around before he spoke. She inhaled, realizing that he thought the room was bugged. She choked on the water, wheezed and coughed. He reached behind her and turned off the water, then stood naked. For her part, she was soaked and dripping. "Take your clothes off," he told her.

"I—"

"I'm not sleeping with you like that."

"Then don't sleep with me."

"Never mind. I'll take them off for you."

He would do it; she knew that now. She had learned that he fought every battle he threatened, so she stared at him in stony silence, then drew the sodden shirt over her head and dropped it to the floor of the tub. Then she stepped out of the skirt. He was still staring at her, his nearness unbearable.

"And the rest," he told her.

She was shaking, furious, afraid. His flesh was but an inch away. Rivulets of water dripped silently down the bronze ridges of his muscles and the expanse of his chest. Her fingers trembled as she reached for the hook to her bra, and he turned her around and released it. She could feel him behind her. She wanted to pretend that this was all a horrible nightmare. He felt so familiar. She wanted to believe that she could throw herself into his arms, and that he would protect her, care for her. Worse, she wanted to make love with him as they had made love before. The kind of lovemaking that made her forget there was a world around her.

No! But she slipped out of the lace bikini panties, then stepped from the tub, wringing out her hair. He didn't stop her as she grabbed one of the thin white towels.

He stepped out of the tub, too, and reached for the second towel. Amber fled, but she heard his movements as he wrung out their clothing and hung it in the bathroom.

Amber sat wrapped in her towel at the foot of the bed, looking at her hands. Michael came into the room, dropped his towel and slid into the bed, pulling the covers over him. She wondered briefly where he had put the gun.

As if reading her mind, he said, "Don't go for it again, Amber. I really don't want to hurt you."

"I want *you* to die," she told him softly.

"I may oblige you," he said. "You should eat."

She glanced at the tray on the dresser. "I'm not hungry."

"Suit yourself." He rolled over, turning his back to her. After a few minutes of silence, she stood; she was going to find the gun.

He wasn't asleep. His voice came out of the darkness. "If you're not hungry, come to bed. If you make one more move for that gun, I'll tie you to this bed. Understand?"

She understood all too clearly. With the towel still wrapped around her, she crawled under the covers. For endless hours she stared into the night.

Then she slept.

She woke with the scent of him rich in her nostrils. For long moments, it seemed right. They had made love; they had fallen asleep. It was nice to sleep together. They hadn't had that chance aboard the *Alexandria*.

She opened her eyes and discovered that she had dislodged her towel during the night. She was curled against him, her chin resting on his chest, her breasts pressed tight to his side, her leg flung over him. Her thigh lay against something that was hard and hot and growing.

She inhaled sharply. They hadn't made love and fallen asleep together—he was a member of the Death Squad, and she had somehow ended up against him during the night. And she was still provocatively pressed against him, with his ardor rising rapidly.

She sprang away from him, then realized that he had been awake, that he had watched her. Color suffused her cheeks, and she started to leap up, but she couldn't find the towel to cover herself. She didn't know if it was better to be naked and away from him, or blanketed but next to him.

"Good morning," he told her and solved the dilemma by crawling over her and out of bed. He pulled open a dresser drawer and took out clean clothing, jeans and a cotton shirt. He dressed, then dug into the drawer again and tossed her a long-sleeved shirt with huge long tails. "Put it on," he told her.

She did so, quickly. She buttoned the buttons, watching his back as he slid a belt through his jeans. "How long do you intend to keep me here?" she demanded.

"With any luck, you'll be out very soon."

"And the senator?"

"He's fine."

"How do I know that?"

"You'll have to take my word for it."

"And why the hell should I do that?" she asked bitterly.

He exhaled slowly. "Because you have no choice." He walked into the bathroom, slammed the door, then emerged a moment later. He picked up her untouched dinner tray, unlocked the door and left.

Amber hugged her knees to her chest. She'd lain beside him for two nights and he hadn't really touched her, not even after the way they had awakened this morning. Maybe the idea of rape was anathema to him, but that still didn't make him a decent man.

She couldn't trust him. He was one of *them*.

She stood and wandered into the bathroom. She was scrubbing her face at the sink when she heard the door open again. She hurried out, afraid, her heart pounding. It was Michael, and despite herself, she was relieved. He'd come back with a tray. There were a coffeepot and two cups, along with rolls and butter and jam. He set the tray on the dresser and poured coffee for both of them. He offered her a cup, and she walked over and accepted it. He buttered her a roll, then handed that to her, too.

Amazingly, a dry half smile came to her features. "What, no jelly?"

He arched a brow and reached for the roll. "Hand it back."

He added jelly to the roll. She was famished, and when he handed her the roll, she wolfed it down, then sipped her coffee and wandered to the bed with it, sitting primly on the edge. "What's going to happen to me, Michael?"

"You'll be home in no time."

"You're lying."

"I'm not."

"You're part of the Death Squad. You're going to make some preposterous demand on the U.S. government, and when they don't comply, you're going to start killing hostages."

"It won't come to that."

He was lying. She knew she'd hit it right. Right on the head.

"You're a liar."

He walked slowly to her and took the cup from her hand. A scream welled in her throat as he threaded his fingers through her hair, forcing her back on the bed and following her down. His lips touched her ear, his whisper so low that she barely heard his words. "It won't come to that if you don't make it come to that. Stay quiet. And for God's sake, don't let them know who you are. If they knew you were Larkspur's daughter, you could be first on the chopping block."

He pushed himself away from her, rose and left the room. She heard the key twist in the lock.

An hour later she had company. A man she thought was called Mohammed came to the door. By then her borrowed Mexican clothing was just about dry, and she felt fairly decent, except for the fact that she was barefoot. Still, when the door opened, she found herself cowering against the wall.

"Ali will speak with you now," he told her.

Her heart thundered. Did he suspect something? What did he want to speak to her about? Mohammed watched her gravely. "He means you no harm, and neither do I."

She followed Mohammed out of the room and down the hallway. She wondered again where Ian Daldrin might be, but there seemed little she could do to discover his whereabouts.

She was surprised when Mohammed led her through the large, sparsely furnished central room and toward the back of the complex. They came to a door, and he opened it for her. It led outside to a grotto in the rocks, with benches and fountains and hanging orchids in many varieties and colors. The mountains rose up on either side, but Amber noted that there were several trails in the foliage that led higher, and one that led down—to the beach?

"Sit, please," Ali said. He was in his burnoose and sunglasses, and he seated himself at a round concrete garden table. There was a bottle of mineral water before him, along with a tray of cheese and fresh fruit. He indicated that she should sit across from him. "Miss... Amber, join me. I'm afraid my tastes are spartan—wine is forbidden in my religion—but you are welcome to what you would like."

"I don't care for wine."

Mohammed had remained standing. Ali gestured, and the man stepped forward and poured a glass of the mineral water for Amber. She sipped it, watching Ali uneasily.

"You live in Washington?"

"Yes."

"And you know Mr. Adams. I'm very sorry that you are so disappointed in him."

"He's a terrorist."

"He's a warrior for justice."

Amber was surprised at how calm she felt. She knew that he had ordered many cold-blooded executions, yet, curiously, she felt that he was—at the least—a fanatic with true beliefs. He would only hurt her if he felt it was truly necessary for his goals. She smiled when she faced him. "Ali, I am sorry. I cannot see that the murder of innocents can be war for justice."

"Because you come from a different world. Because you have never had to fight for the land of your fathers. You have not seen the raw and brutal terror in some Central American lands when the new rebels fight the old rebels, and the dictators order the deaths of thousands. I have done what is necessary to prove that I am a force that must be heard."

Amber shook her head. "What you do is murder. And you order other men to do murder. You order them to die themselves."

"And they will sit at the right hand of Allah."

"It isn't necessary! And it isn't so simple. I happen to know a large number of Muslims, and they don't—"

She broke off, because he was staring at her intently.

"How do you come to know so many of my religion?"

Because she was her father's daughter, she thought fleetingly. She had traveled with him as a child to many Middle East countries, and she had been seated at endless dinners with diplomats and ambassadors. "I went to school with a number of Turkish children," she lied. Then she found herself facing him again. "And we got on very well together! They were kind and gentle people."

"Americanized," came a voice from behind Amber. She swung around. Khazar had come into the garden from one of the trails. He wore an automatic rifle over his shoulder and began to speak to his father in Arabic. Ali seemed troubled by his son's appearance. He answered in English, looking at Amber. "I enjoy hearing about the lives of others." He waved his hand in the air. Khazar cast Amber a cold glance, then turned and left them.

Ali leaned forward. "You like Washington?"

She nodded. "I love it. I love the cherry blossoms in the spring, and the parks and the monuments. And the Smithsonian—"

"Yes, yes, I would love to see the Smithsonian. I receive the magazine—"

"You what?"

"Well, not here, of course!" Ali laughed. "It is sent to me in France. I read the articles. I imagine that I can see the vast displays, the spaceships, the animals. I would most like, I think, to see the Museum of the American People."

"Really?"

"Yes."

He went on to tell her about his first trip to a museum in Cairo when he had been a boy, and how the endless rooms of mummies had terrified, then fascinated him. He talked with vigor and a thirst for knowledge that startled and somewhat seduced her. When he had finished, she realized that she had eaten a handful of grapes and an orange and a few large chunks of cheese.

Then Mohammed interrupted him courteously, and Ali sighed. "I have enjoyed our conversation. I hope that you will be returned to Washington soon enough."

He rose, and Mohammed nodded, indicating that he would return her to her room.

Ali was already walking away. She called out to him. "Please! Wait!" He turned. "Please, just let us go. The senator and me. And I know you must be holding other Americans. The government can't help us, you must understand that. There are courts of law—"

"I'm sorry. I see what my destiny demands of me, and I must follow it." He hesitated. "I have seen that more clothes have been brought to your room." He hesitated again. "I heard your screams the other night, but it is not right for one man to interfere with another man and his woman. Unless it is a lie. Unless Michael has made this up, and there is nothing between you. I can have you taken from him."

She inhaled sharply. She wanted to shout, yes! But the word would not come. She was far more afraid of Khazar than she was of Michael. She couldn't help believing that he did want her to survive. And she knew that whatever stress and humiliation he put her through, he would not attack her. In addition, he had warned her not to let Ali know she was Ted Larkspur's daughter.

"Miss . . . ?" Ali addressed her.

"Taylor," she said quickly. "Amber Taylor."

"Michael asked me to watch over you in his absence. No one will disturb you again while he is gone. But even he will not disturb you, if that is your choice."

She lowered her head. "No. I thank you, but leave me with Michael, please."

He nodded and left, walking down the trail his son had taken earlier. Mohammed motioned to her, and she followed him.

Michael did not return to the room until very late. Ali had indeed ordered that clothes should be left for her. She had been given a pair of jeans and several shirts.

The man she thought was named Jaime brought her dinner. It was lamb, nicely cooked and well-seasoned, with carrots and potatoes. She ate, determined that she was going to maintain her health. She would either manage to escape, or she would be a fine specimen when she was killed.

When the hour grew late, she curled against the wall. She heard Michael come in, but she pretended not to. He didn't disturb her, merely lay down beside her.

In the morning, when she awakened, he was already gone, but a tray with coffee and rolls was waiting for her. She ate and showered and dressed nervously in a shirt and jeans.

She saw no one for hours and had begun to doze when she heard the key in the lock. It was Mohammed. "Ali will see you," he said.

Amber nodded. She accompanied him to the orchid garden, where the old man awaited her once again. She took her seat before him and started the conversation by telling him that she really couldn't converse with a terrorist. He explained to her that he was not a terrorist, and they were once more cast into an interesting debate. Before she knew it, she was again conversing.

"Violence with no purpose is a crime," he assured her.

"Blowing up airplanes isn't?"

"When there is war, many men die."

"Infants die in airplanes. Mothers with little children."

"Children grow up to be warriors. We have learned that lesson well."

"Children should not die."

"The world is not a perfect place."

He again asked her about the Smithsonian. She found herself answering him, and they talked with surprising ease all through lunch. Afterward, feeling she had to know, she said, "I want to know how Senator Daldrin is."

Ali nodded. "Fair enough." He stood and nodded to Mohammed, then walked with her into the complex. She was somewhat alarmed when he led her down a hallway with numerous armed guards. They came to a door with a small, square window. "You may look quickly," he told her.

She looked in and gasped.

The senator was in the room, seated at the foot of a bed. The room looked like a hospital room. It was very large, but it housed several men.

At least they were all alive. And they seemed to be well enough. One was smoking a cigar and talking with Daldrin. Across the room, a few others were playing poker. Their confinement might be tense and harrowing as they awaited their fates, but at least they were not being starved or tortured.

Ali tugged on her arm, pulling her gently away from the window. "They are well, as you can see."

"Yes."

"Mohammed will take you back now."

Ali remained in the hallway as Mohammed led Amber away. When she looked back, Ali was still standing there.

When they came to the central area, Mohammed paused. Khazar was there, armed, talking to Jaime and Juan. He had chosen English instead of Spanish, and Amber thought that perhaps he had learned that language better than the other.

"It is done. Our demands have been stated. On the Fourth of July, there will be fireworks."

He turned around and saw Amber, saw the ashen pallor of her face. He smiled. "A woman. We will save her for last, eh, my friends?"

No one laughed. At least they felt some pity for her, she thought.

The Fourth of July. It was now June 18. There was very little time to go.

Khazar shrugged and turned away, striding down the hall in the direction she had left his father. When Jaime and Juan followed him, Mohammed said beneath his breath, "Excuse me. Wait one moment."

To Amber's amazement, the man left her standing and followed Khazar. She looked around. The place was secure. Ali had numerous men, numerous weapons. This place had once been a Spanish fortress. Guards were posted everywhere.

Where could she go? She was barefoot, and she hadn't the least idea of her actual location.

They were going to start killing people on the Fourth of July.

Amber saw the door to the garden. She glanced around one more time, then ran desperately for the exit. No one stopped her.

She paused in the garden. Two paths led up the mountain, and one led down. To the beach?

She chose the third path and ran.

Chapter 9

Island of the Damned
June 18

Within minutes she was wondering why she had run—it must have been one of the stupidest moves of her life. Her feet were bare, and every step she took brought some new torture as she sped over the trail. There were pebbles and rocks beneath her feet, and roots from the endless trees. The vegetation slapped her cruelly in the face, branches seemed to reach out to try to catch her, to hold her, like the dry and brittle fingers of a phantom captor.

She hadn't the least idea of where she was going. And they would be after her very soon.

She had to stop. She had to catch her breath. The gasping sound of it was awful to her own ears, like the raging of a thunderstorm. Her lungs felt as if they would burst, and her calves ached in a million places.

She didn't dare look at the soles of her feet; she could feel the trickle of blood escaping from her toes.

She stopped, bending over, bracing her hands on her knees and looking back. So far, no one was coming. Maybe they thought that she was wandering around the complex. Maybe they hadn't noticed she was missing yet. It didn't matter. When they discovered her disappearance, they would come after her. She had to keep moving.

She was probably leaving a trail as clear as written directions, but she had little choice. All she could do was run.

She started off again. Within minutes she realized that she had strayed from the true path, that she was trying to move through a thick net of brush. The farther along she went, the fewer trees she encountered, and the denser the brush became. The ground beneath her feet began to change, becoming grainier. Sandier. And the incline down which she ran became steeper.

She swore, picking up a burr in her toe. She paused to pluck it out, and winced at the raw appearance of her feet. How much longer was she going to be able to go on before the pain caused her to scream, and then hobble to some bush, fall down beside it and sob like an idiot?

She had to keep going. Downward was the sea, and her only chance of escape.

She turned to look back again. She saw nothing but the endless green of the tropical jungle, the color becoming softer now with the coming of twilight. It would be dark soon. Would that be in their favor—or hers? Probably theirs. They were jungle fighters. The only darkness she knew or welcomed was when she was safely curled up with her head on a down pillow in bed for the night.

She moved on, crying out when she ran straight into a huge spiderweb. Nearly hysterical, she clawed the clinging web from her face, inhaling, bringing it into her mouth, blowing it out again, stumbling along as she did so.

She turned too late. Just as she swept the sticky remnants of the spider's web from her lips and lashes, she saw that the ground had all but disappeared before her. Her feet slid out from under her, and she landed hard on her rump.

She began to roll, but she realized quickly that she wasn't going to be able to stop her descent down the steep incline. She covered her face with her hands and went with the motion as best she could. Leaves slapped at her, branches scratched her arms and hands. Then she opened her eyes in time to see the dark and mysterious world as she catapulted forward . . . seemed to fly . . . and landed, stunned and soaked, in a pool of water.

It wasn't deep. And there was sand beneath her feet. The water was temperate but salty, and she assumed that it had to connect with the sea. Struggling to her feet, she looked around.

The mountains rose immediately before her, their jagged peaks stretching far to the right. She was on a plateau, probably very near sea level. She could see nothing but brush when she twisted to look behind her, but it seemed that there was a break far to her right, where the water trickled and tumbled to some destination below.

She smoothed her hair and stumbled onto the sand. Where the earth rose again, she realized, there were caves. She stared that way through the growing darkness as she sat on the sand, bathing her stinging feet in the water. Did she stand a chance of moving with night almost upon her? Should she take refuge in a cave until morning, when she could see again? Her slide down the mountain had brought her here. A second slide could send her tumbling down to solid rock, or shafts of coral.

She hesitated, squinting and trying to fathom the direction of the water's flow. The entire island was Ali Abdul's, she thought. The fishermen were probably on his payroll, along with anyone else who inhabited the place. They were not, at the very least, a people friendly to the U.S. government—unless some Central American coup had taken place in the past few days.

Despair nearly overwhelmed her. Where could she possibly go, even if she survived the night without recapture? She could steal a boat, with luck—if she wasn't shot in the process. Then she would have to navigate the coral reefs and the shoals, and then she would be in the open Caribbean, without a notion in hell of how to reach a safe port.

What were her alternatives? she asked herself dryly. Ali had liked her—but that was before she had caused trouble. And his demands on the U.S. government were preposterous—they couldn't possibly release convicted assassins. If she was captured, she would await her day to die—with the others. If she could make good her escape, perhaps there was a prayer of rescue for them all.

There was a sudden rumble of sound behind her. Forgetting her sore feet, Amber leaped up and swung around. Someone was coming. Someone was coming just the same way she had come, sliding down the incline. There was a huge splash, and the water thundered and roared as a body made contact with it.

Amber let out a yelp and turned to race along the sand. In the dusk she could barely see. She almost headed into the caves that had once hinted of safe harbor. Now they could mean entrapment. Her only chance was to reach that narrow strip where the sand and water seemed to pitch downward again. Perhaps there was a treacherous fall ahead, but it seemed that there was certain death behind her.

Her feet pounded on the sand. Then she tripped on a rock, fell and started rolling. She could hear the water beside her, falling down the incline just as she was.

Then she could hear the sound of pounding feet, someone who had not fallen as she had, but who now pursued her with agility and stealth, coming ever nearer.

She came to a plateau and managed to stumble to her feet, but she was tackled from behind and sent flying facedown into the sand. It filled her mouth, and she gasped and spat. She could barely breathe; hysteria was settling in. She twisted, fighting with the strength and desperation of a madwoman. She kicked and shoved with her knee, and heard a wicked groan. Her damp hair tangled over her eyes so she couldn't see her captor; she could only imagine the outcome of his victory over her. She would surely be bloodied and broken; retaliation would be savage.

Her arms flailed, her fingernails digging. She choked and cried out as her wrists were caught. "No, no, no!" she screamed, thrashing against the hold. Both her wrists were secured high above her head. She opened her mouth to scream, and a hand clamped down hard upon it. A whisper sounded against her cheek as a body lay hard over hers.

"Amber, stop! Listen to me. It's Michael."

It was Michael. So he would not hurt her now; instead he would drag her back, and Khazar would make certain she was hurt.

She tried her best to bite his hand, and she twisted again, trying to kick. His hold on her was too strong, and she felt his muscles constrict still more tightly as she struggled. She was never going to be able to move. Tears burned behind her lids, then spilled past her lashes. She had fought so hard.

And she had believed so deeply in this man, only to find him the instrument of her ultimate destruction.

"Amber." His voice was very soft, husky, persuasive. "Amber, please, listen to me. You can't scream. The men have been given the okay to shoot to kill if I can't bring you in. I want to take my hand off your mouth, but you can't scream."

She didn't believe him; she didn't trust him. She wanted to throw her arms around him and believe in him again, but she didn't dare. She must be losing her mind. She was so desperate that she wanted to put her hand into the hand of her enemy.

"Amber..."

Slowly, his palm lifted from her lips, and she inhaled deeply. His weight was still securely on her. "Amber, please, I'm going to try to help you."

"I don't believe you!" she whispered fervently. "I don't believe you. You're one of them. You've caused this. You're part of a damned stupid holy war—"

"I'm not part of a holy war," he interrupted her. She fell silent. "Listen to me," he said very quietly. "I'm here to try to get them all out."

"What?" Amber said.

He released her wrists, warning her to silence as he smoothed her hair. She could just make out his rugged features in the pale light of the rising moon. "Amber, it was the only way. You weren't supposed to be part of it."

"Michael, what are you talking about?"

"My name isn't Michael. Well, it is. It just isn't Michael Adams. It's Adam Michael Tchartoff."

"What?" Her mind was reeling. What in God's name was he saying? What was he telling her? And did it make any difference? Could she believe anything he said? She shook her head suddenly, tears rising to her eyes again. "Don't lie to me now. I beg you, for the love of God, don't lie to me now. You don't need to. You have me. You can rape me, kill me, cut me into little pieces. Just don't lie to me anymore."

"I never meant to lie to you!" he said harshly, his voice rising. "I meant to stay away from you, far away from you."

"Who are you?" Her voice was rising, too. His hand fell over her mouth again, and he leaned close.

"Stay quiet. Voices carry here. I'll try to give it to you quickly, in a nutshell. I was minding my own business when I was summoned to Washington and asked to infiltrate the Death Squad. I've worked intelligence before and already had the perfect alter ego to work with, a man named Michael Adams. A character with a shady background, but also a reputation for excellence. The type of man any faction might want on their side. It would have been impossible for me to infiltrate as Adam Tchartoff—he's known in certain circles, too."

"Who summoned you?" Amber interrupted.

He hesitated, staring at her. "Your father."

"I don't believe you."

"You don't want to believe me, but it's the truth. And he didn't have any choice. They knew about this island, but what were they going to do, declare war? All of North, South and Central America, along with half of Europe and the Middle East, and maybe even Russia, would have wound up at war, too. Terrorists aren't easy to fight, in case you haven't noticed. The president gives the orders, so don't blame your father because he studies men well and came up with the proper name."

"Why?" Amber demanded.

He shrugged. "I had my reasons."

"Senator Daldrin—"

"Senator Daldrin knew he was the target. He was willing to be taken."

Amber stared at him. She wanted to believe him. She wanted to believe him so much.

"But—"

"Amber, I had to get on the island. Then, during the past few days, I had to do my best to study the terrain and the compound. I had to get down to the open end of the island and meet with a certain fisherman—"

"A fisherman!"

"Amber, I told you, the United States knows we're here. And they have other people close to the inside, too."

"What are you saying?"

"Explosives were sent here. I've been wiring the compound, the weapons stores, everything, so I can blow the place up when we escape."

"You're going to blow up the entire island?"

He shook his head. "No. Don't you see? There are people who live here. Not exactly innocents, but they aren't murderers. They're just common people trying to eke out their existence. One dictator comes and goes, a new regime is in and the old one is out. It makes little difference to them. The members of the Death Squad come here, and they have guns, and they're very powerful, and they leave the people alone. But still, it would hurt the United States to make war on them, do you understand?"

She nodded very slowly, staring at him. She wondered if he had lost his mind, or if she had lost hers. Or maybe it was all true. She wanted to explode, she was so furious, but the moment she opened her mouth she fell silent, for he pressed a warning finger against her lips. The jungle had ears. He didn't want to be found.

Still, she lashed out against him, but quietly. "Why didn't you tell me? If you are this Adam Tchartoff person, why didn't you tell me? Why didn't you warn me?"

"When?" he whispered. "On the ship? On the island? Before or after making love? I kept telling you to stay away from me. I couldn't give you my real name. I couldn't give away anything. This was a top-secret mission. Only Daldrin knew what was going to happen. We didn't dare blow it. Then you came along and blew it anyway. Why didn't you run? Why did you have to stand there on deck screaming like some damn movie heroine?"

It was difficult to be indignant when he was straddling her hips, holding her prisoner. Even in the moonlight, his eyes were ice-blue, and so cold. All around them was darkness, shadows, the furtive, secretive rustlings of the tropical jungle. And there was the whisper and bubble of the water as it cascaded by them, strangely beautiful in the night. Yet it was a sound that warned her it wasn't over, that they had come to a perilous Eden here, and she still might never leave it. She fought against the pounding of her heart and said, her voice soft, defying him, "I had to scream. What did you expect me to do, let those men kidnap a statesman and a friend?"

He rose, reaching down to her. When his fingers closed around hers, she found that she was trembling. Things were coming out into the open, and all that she could think of was the past. She wanted to believe him, but was it only because she wanted to believe him? Because he had yet to really hurt her? Because he hadn't forced anything from her, even when he had her completely in his power?

Or because he had never seemed to care enough about anything or anyone to lie? His name was not Michael, it was Adam. Adam Tchartoff. And he was more of an enigma now than ever.

She still didn't trust him; she *couldn't* trust him. By his own admission, he had brought Daldrin here on purpose and her by accident. He was a spy, he had told her. A spy on behalf of his country.

She stared at his hand, at the strong, bronzed fingers, the callused palm. She accepted it, and he pulled her to her feet. Their eyes met, and she watched him suspiciously. Her voice very low, she asked him, "If you are who you say you are, why did my father pretend not to know who I was talking about the day of the memorial service? Why did Daldrin want you around me all the time—and yet not want us to be alone together? Think about it—Mr. Tchartoff. Doesn't that make you look like a rather suspicious character?"

"Your father and Daldrin were concerned for you, I imagine."

"If you're an American, why wouldn't they accept you?'"

"I'm not an American. Not anymore."

She pulled her hand away from his. "Then what are you?"

"An Israeli."

It was all so fantastic. She didn't know what to believe. And he didn't seem to feel the need to convince her any longer. He turned and started walking up the

incline toward the caves. She hurried after him, forgetting the need to be silent, forgetting everything in
a sudden burst of fury.

She caught hold of his arm, spinning him around
furiously. "You told me it wasn't a holy war! You told
me—"

"I told you to shut up!" he warned her, catching her
shoulders. He opened his mouth to speak, then fell
silent, dragging her to the ground. She started to protest, then heard the rustle of brush high above them,
a rustle that indicated men tramping around.

Her heart beat faster. As he held her, she could feel
his heartbeat matching her own, just as their breath
and the tension within fused until they were one.

"She isn't here, and she hasn't been here!" someone said in accented English.

"She must be on the island," came the reply. The
second speaker was Mohammed, Amber was certain,
and they were speaking in English because his Spanish was so limited, and apparently the other man's
Arabic was just as poor.

"No, she doesn't have to be on the island!" the first
man retorted. "That Adam, that genius with explosives, that priceless fool, he may have taken her. He is
more in love with the woman than he is with any
cause! We should have killed her. We should have
killed her that night on the ship!"

The other man said something that neither Amber
nor Adam could hear. Then the voices faded away,
and the soft, subtle jungle noises took over once again.

They waited. Silent, perfectly still, their heartbeats
gradually slowing together. And while they waited,

Amber suddenly knew beyond a doubt that it was true, it was all true, every word he had told her. A rush of warmth swept over her as she realized that he wasn't a terrorist, that he didn't want to murder men in cold blood, that they were, in a strange way, on the same side. She closed her eyes, feeling the night, feeling his hands on her, still holding her close. She'd been falling in love with him on the ship. She'd never known what force of nature had made her so desperately attracted to him, and she didn't know what it was that had so seeped into her heart that she'd wanted to forgive him, no matter what. At least now she knew she wasn't a fool, that her intuition about him had been right. Maybe it didn't matter, of course, because they still might die. And perhaps there was more, because he hadn't answered all her questions. There was still a wall there, a wall that warned her to stay away. It hadn't been only a question of security; he hadn't wanted her to come close.

His hold on her eased, and he got slowly to his feet. Once again he reached down to her, but he was gazing up the mountainside and spoke softly. "They're on to me." He looked at her, his eyes the shade of the night-touched moon. "We'll stay here tonight, in the caves. They won't search again until light, and I'll head in at dawn."

"Head in! You can't go back! They'll kill you."

"I have to go back. I'm not done setting the fuses, and more important than that, I've got to get Daldrin and the others out."

"But—"

"Amber," he said, taking her shoulders fiercely again, "this is as safe a place as you're going to find. The falls lead to the mouth of the river, and at eleven tomorrow morning, there will be American boats right off the shore. If I don't come back, ride the river. Follow it out to the ocean. You'll make it."

"What do you mean, if you don't come back?"

He released her impatiently and started up the incline. She didn't follow him, and he looked at her. "Come on. Let's find shelter in the caves."

She thought about ignoring his order, but that wouldn't ease her frustration. She followed him, almost slipping on the steep, damp incline. He must have heard her falter, because he turned, took her hand and led her the rest of the way up. They stood before one of the caves, a trickle of water falling from above. He started to say something, then looked down silently. His eyes met hers, and he reached out, sweeping her into his arms. She almost cried out, startled, but swallowed the sound. He took her to the bed of the river, where he knelt with her and carefully bathed her feet. She stared at his tawny head and remained silent. He ripped off the tails of his cotton shirt and bound them gently around her feet, then lifted her and carried her into the cave.

"They must hurt like blazes," he said.

She didn't answer him. There was little light, so she could barely see him. And there was so much that she wanted to know about him. She reached up and touched his cheek. "What was your first language?" she asked him.

His eyes fell to meet hers. "Russian."

"Russian!"

He smiled at last, a rueful smile. And he walked deeper into the cave, where he set her against the wall, then sat beside her. "I can't light a fire," he told her. "It would lead them straight to us."

"I don't need a fire. Michael—Adam. I need to know something about you," she said.

He shrugged. His wrists rested upon his knees, his hands dangling until he lifted them, then let them fall again. "My father was a Russian refugee after the war. My mother was Austrian, but she had been in a concentration camp, and even by 1950, when I was born, the Austrian government was still so swamped with refugees that they weren't allowing the children born of other nationalities to become citizens. We managed to reach the United States, and I became an American."

"Oh." He hadn't really explained a thing. But he was still smiling in the darkness; she knew him well enough now to read his features by the tone of his voice. Sometimes. When he wanted to be read, she thought.

"My father died, and my mother moved to Israel. I joined her there." His smile faded. She wanted to touch him, but she couldn't. A coldness was suddenly emanating from him, and though she desperately wanted him to go on, she didn't know if she wanted to hear what he had to say.

"I met a woman. An Israeli woman. I fell in love, and we married, and we had a child, and I became an Israeli."

His coldness settled over her heart. He had a wife and a child, and everything he had shared with her had been an awful, horrible lie.

"You have a wife and a child," she whispered. "And yet you've come here to risk your life—"

"They're dead," he said flatly. "And I am already dead, Miss Amber Larkspur, and so I risk my life. They died because of a car bomb. It was meant for the army intelligence officer Adam Tchartoff, but it killed a beautiful young woman and an innocent baby girl. It was set by the Death Squad at the command of Khazar Abdul, and that is also why I am here. I could never tell you any of this before because I was afraid you might give me away, you were so frantic. But that's it now, everything."

Everything. And she felt colder than ever. "At the memorial service that day—"

"I came to the memorial service because I served with the unit. It was your father's way of contacting me. That service was arranged so he could reach me."

"My father wouldn't—"

"Your father didn't do anything wrong. He needed to contact me, and the service was a good thing. It wasn't a lie. You were there. It was good for the widows and the children and the men. He accomplished two things at once, that's all."

"He told me to stay away from you."

"Yes." He stretched out by the wall without saying more. Amber stood uncertainly and moved a short distance away from him. She stretched out and stared at the ceiling, wondering how she could still be in such grave danger, yet lie there aching anew for what she felt she had lost. "Tell me," she whispered in the darkness, "did I mean anything to you at all?"

He was silent for a long moment. Then he said, just as quietly. "Yes. You meant everything. I was alive again."

Alive... But he made no move to touch her, and the tenor of his voice had not changed. She had hated him, had fought him for betraying her. But he had never betrayed her. And she wanted to go to him tonight because she might never be able to again. She had slept beside him, afraid of the warmth of his flesh and the power of his limbs, but her fears had been groundless. And now they had only the few hours until dawn. She didn't know if he loved her—if he ever *could* love her—but she was sorry for his pain.

And she needed to touch him.

She rose in the darkness, but this time she did not move away from him. She walked to his side, and she knew he was aware that she had come, but he didn't move. He only waited. She got down on her knees beside him, and the filtering moonlight allowed her to see the strong lines of his features and the light-blue fire of his eyes. She opened her mouth to speak, but the words refused to come. She unbuttoned her shirt, pulled it over her head and let it fall to the floor, and still he didn't say anything, didn't move, his eyes surveying her. "I—I need you, Adam," she managed to stutter at last. "I need you tonight. Please..."

Her voice lingered on the air. She was afraid that he wouldn't touch her, that the truth, the pain, bare and exposed, might sweep him away from her. "Adam..."

His arms swept around her, drawing her down, her lips hovering over his. "Adam, may I stay? I need you so badly tonight. I need to touch you and hold you and . . ."

He smiled, and the blue fire rose into his eyes. "There is a word in my mother's country. *Shalom.* Welcome. I need you, too," he whispered in turn. And then his lips touched her, fusing with them in a hot, open-mouthed kiss that stole into her soul and swept her breath away.

The cave floor was cold and damp, and the night was filled with danger, yet none of that mattered. His touch was the fire against the cold. Amber heard the flow of the water, the melody moving beyond the cave. She heard the magic of the night, the chirping of the crickets, the call of the birds. And she heard the echoes of their hearts, and the breeze that swept around them. They were on their feet, facing one another, and their clothing was gone. And there, in the moonlight, Amber stood before him and thought that they might have been alone together in some strange, exotic paradise. Adam might have been the first man, his skin glowing in the pale light that filtered into the cave, the length of him hard and masculine, the call between them as ancient as the earth beneath them. Welcome. He wanted her tonight. She felt the heat of his gaze and knew that his eyes were sweeping over her, and that he found her beautiful despite her salt-dampened hair and rag-wrapped feet. When he looked at her that way, the danger of the night disappeared and they were alone in Eden.

She cried out softly, and together they closed the space between them. Suddenly she was in his arms again. He caressed her shoulders and held her close as his lips met hers once more, as his tongue moved into her mouth. He made love aggressively, givingly, but tonight *she* was going to touch *him*.

She broke the kiss, then tasted his lips, teasing them with her tongue. Then her mouth moved to his shoulders, to his chest. With slow, sensual desire, she moved her body against his. She teased his nipples with her teeth and nuzzled her face lower against the crisp, tawny hairs on his chest. She touched him, her touch moving lower, until she was on her knees before him. She loved him completely, and he, too, got down on his knees before her, wrapping her in his arms.

When they lay down on the hard earth she felt as if her bed was in the clouds, because sensation ruled her heart and her senses. All that she wanted was this man deep inside her. He entered her with hunger, with fierce, compelling desire. He moved in rhythm with the pulse of the night, with the tempest of the falls, with hot, driving passion. The crashing of the water seemed to escalate; the drumbeat of the night came harder and harder. His muscles strained and tightened, tension constricting his body, tightening his features. She felt the earth, and yet she wasn't of it. Soft sounds escaped her as she rose so high it seemed unbearable, and then the shimmering explosion of ultimate sensation came upon her, and the ecstasy of it freed them from danger, brought them from darkness into brilliant, bursting gold light.

He held her close, their hearts beating in unison, slowing in unison. Amber groaned and turned her head into his shoulder, where she softly kissed his salt-damp skin and lay replete.

She didn't know how long they were still. She heard the movement of the water, felt the gentle breezes of the night cooling their naked flesh. But then his fingers threaded into her hair, massaging her nape, and he lifted her head and whispered softly, "You make me feel alive again, Amber." Then he groaned and kissed her again, and she felt the heat rising within him once more.

She never knew when his soothing touch became the touch of passion. The night was short, but there were hours there to be shared. Sleep was forgotten. Again and again the precious sweetness exploded within her, and then his lips would touch hers once more, his hand would cradle her breast, and his lips would be hot against the coolness of her flesh, until the need rose all over again. Finally she realized that when the brilliance fell upon them, it was the real light of dawn.

Adam rose and went to the lagoon, and Amber knew that no matter what they had shared during the night, the day had come to rob them of it.

When he returned, he dressed quietly. She watched him with her eyes half closed, and he stared at her. Then he lowered himself to his knees beside her once again. "Stay here," he whispered to her. "And don't forget. If I'm not back by eleven o'clock, you start out. Follow the river and swim like a champ. Do you understand?"

She flung her arms around him. "Don't leave me here alone. Let me come—"

"You would be in my way, and God knows, if someone got his hands on you, it could be the death of all of us. We both know that. You have to stay here, and don't leave the cave. Do you understand? Don't leave the cave. I don't want to see you."

She nodded against his chest. "But I can't do it. I can't let you go."

"You have to," he told her.

"If you go back—"

"I have to go back. You know that."

He released her quickly and walked purposefully out of the cave. She knew that he was gone for good.

Amber reached for her shirt, shivering as she slipped into it. She saw that he had scratched out a message in the sand. *Shalom.* He had forgotten to remind her last night that it also meant goodbye.

She rose and climbed into her jeans. Her hands and face were hot and dusty and sticky, and without thought, she hobbled out of the cave toward the water. She shouldn't drink the brackish water, she knew, no matter how thirsty she was. Still, she dampened her feet in their bindings, and splashed water over her face. She froze then, remembering that he had told her not to leave the cave. But when she looked around quickly, she couldn't see a thing.

She heard a rustle in the brush, and her heart thundered, then seemed to stop, and she waited, still and silent, but she saw no one. The sun was beginning to beat down. The world was green and blue and, according to all apparent evidence, peaceful.

She went to the cave and waited, wondering if she would have the courage to go down the river if he didn't come back.

She glanced at her wristwatch. The elegant gold tones seemed so out of place with her ill-fitting jeans, men's cotton shirt, rag-wrapped feet and salt-encrusted hair. It was a testament to the manufacturer's skill that the timepiece was still working, she reflected. Or was it? Time seemed to be crawling by. Seconds ticked by more slowly than whole days.

She paced the floor, then sat for a while again. It wasn't even eight-thirty, but it felt as if Adam had been gone for hours. How had she come to this? Maybe God played tricks on people. Maybe he had brought her Adam just to show her that she had never really known what she wanted before, that she hadn't begun to understand love.

Not that he had ever said he loved her. He undoubtedly didn't love her. He had been fiercely in love with his wife, the woman who had died.

But I made him feel alive! she reminded herself wistfully.

He was gone now, though, and she didn't know if she would ever see him again.

She paused suddenly, hearing something outside the cave. A rustle of brush . . . something.

Her hand flew to her throat. Adam. It was over, and he had come back, and she didn't need to worry about going alone. They would be together.

She started to rush for the entrance, then stopped dead still.

Even from the shadows of the cave, she knew immediately that it was not Adam who had come for her. It was Khazar.

And he wasn't alone. Two of his men were with him, flanking him, hovering just outside the entrance to the cave.

Legs spread, hands on his hips, his automatic swinging from his shoulder, he smiled broadly, his teeth flashing in the dim light. "There you are. We've been anxious to find you. All alone out here in the wilderness, as it were. We were completely at a loss, having no idea of where you might have gone until Jaime saw you when he was out on his patrol. I imagine that Tchartoff was here during the night. Yes, Tchartoff. We know his name now. I never wanted him here." Khazar stopped speaking and spat in the sand. "My father was duped by him. My father was soft. But I know Tchartoff's name, and I know, too, that you are Amber Larkspur, and I know who your father is. American newspapers are filled with your picture."

Amber backed against the wall of the cave. Adam had told her not to go outside. He had told her, and she had immediately forgotten, and now Khazar was standing there, and he knew everything.

"Where is Tchartoff?" he demanded.

She shook her head. She really couldn't answer. She didn't know.

"Answer me."

"I don't know where he is."

"But he knows that you are here. He will come back for you."

"No. No, he won't come back."

"I think that he will. I think that I even know how to guarantee that he will."

He strode across the cave toward her. She flattened herself against the stone wall and swung out furiously, managing to land a good blow on his jaw. But he gritted his teeth against the pain and savagely thrust his fingers into her hair, gripping it so tightly that she cried out in pain. "Come, Miss Larkspur. We'll go outside, where we'll give Tchartoff a chance to come. We'll go tell him just what I'm going to do to you if he doesn't step forward quickly."

"No!" she cried out.

His grip was merciless as he dragged her out of the cave despite her desperate protests.

"Your father will not allow this!" she told him.

Dark eyes fell on hers. Cold, evil eyes. He smiled with a curl of his lip. "My father is dead. He died of a heart attack last night, Miss Larkspur. I am in charge now.

"And you, Miss Larkspur, are in very grave trouble."

Chapter 10

Khazar stood with her on the embankment and started to shout. "Tchartoff! Can you hear me, Tchartoff? I'm out here with the woman. She's really important, isn't she? More important than Daldrin, or any of those military men, eh? Ted Larkspur's daughter. You haven't got a choice. You have to come in. I'll kill her, you know I will. I'll take my time. Maybe I'll give her to Juan and then kill her."

He waited. The water continued to rush by, and the breeze lightly rustled the trees.

"Adam, don't come—" Amber began to shout, but Khazar wrenched hard on her hair. Tears stung her eyes, and she fell silent with a sharp gasp of pain.

"He must be at the complex!" Khazar swore suddenly. He didn't release his hold on Amber as he strode toward the incline, where he gripped a tree trunk with his free hand. "Climb!" he ordered her. She had no choice. He was dragging her along, and she could scarcely bear the pain. But neither could she keep up. Her feet were slipping on the damp earth.

One of his men said something, and a second later she was lifted and tossed over the man's shoulder. He knew the terrain well. He was like a mountain goat, easily using the trees for support and managing her weight at the same time.

They reached the plateau at last, and the man set her down. The moment her feet hit the earth, she started to run, but her hair was seized again, and she was slammed hard against Khazar's chest. "No. You will not escape me."

Now she had to walk. He shoved her ahead of him, nudging her in the back with his rifle when she would have paused. She kept going, trying to keep her chin high, trying to ignore the cold steel touching her. It was a long walk, and her feet were killing her.

They came at last to the garden, where Khazar stood up on one of the rocks. "Tchartoff! I've got the woman! I'll give you one hour to get here! Then I'll kill her." He was silent. "After an hour, she will bore me, Tchartoff, do you hear me? After one hour, she dies."

He waited. Amber felt the tension creeping into her muscles as she stood. They were both listening, but the only reply was the silence of the jungle.

Khazar leaped down from the rock, caught hold of Amber's elbow and shoved her forward again. His men followed as they walked into the compound.

Khazar pushed Amber down a hallway and kicked open a door, then shoved her inside.

It was an office and, she thought, his sleeping quarters. There was a very modern desk, and weapons on the wall, swords and daggers and rifles, and long, evil-looking whips.

But there were Persian carpets on the floor, a sofa covered with damask pillows and, in the far corner of the room, a water pipe. A true indulgence for such a man, she thought.

The door closed sharply behind her. She spun around to see that Khazar was in the room with her. He stared at her, and his eyes were dark with hatred.

"Shouldn't you be mourning for your father?" she asked him.

"My father was a fool. I have awaited his death."

"Do the men know you feel that way?"

"What the men know does not matter to you."

She swallowed and backed away from him. He smiled and watched her eyes as she studied the wall. Suddenly he snatched one of the whips and walked toward her. The whip cracked in the air. She felt the cord encircle her neck and grabbed at it. Slowly but inexorably, he drew her closer and closer to him, while she desperately tried to free herself.

She stood before him, and he took up a handful of her hair, rubbing it through his fingers. "What is it he sees that he will die for, eh? Hair like gold? Eyes like the sea? Are you better than other women? Is there magic between your thighs? Should I discover the truth?"

She couldn't move; the whip was too tight around her throat. He drew his free hand along her side, gliding his palm over her breast, cradling her softness. She choked out her indignation, trying to pull away.

He shoved her, unwound the whip cord, then released her so suddenly that she tumbled on the sofa. Smiling, he straddled her, and she swore, trying to knee him. His palm cracked hard against her cheek, and for a moment she saw stars. Then she felt his hand on the bodice of her shirt. A scream bubbled in her throat as she felt his touch upon the bare flesh at her collarbone.

Then the door burst open, and they both started, swinging around.

"Khazar!"

Adam had come. He stood there, eyes narrowed, watching his enemy. He was armed with a heavy pistol, and it was aimed at Khazar.

Khazar smiled his lazy smile and rose, jerking Amber up with him, holding her close. "I have your woman."

"Let her go."

"No. I will kill her if you don't drop the gun. I will snap her neck. You know I can."

"Yes, I know it," Adam said quietly. His mouth was grim, his eyes icy, and he was calm, completely at ease. He waved the gun idly around and sauntered into the room, then leaned casually against the desk. Amber stared at him in amazement. He didn't seem to care in the least that Khazar was threatening her life.

"You killed my wife, Khazar," he said.

Khazar shrugged. She felt his every movement. His elbow was locked around her throat. She had never realized the man's strength before. If he bent his elbow just a bit more, he could snap sinew and bone. "I meant to kill Adam Tchartoff, the great military commander, the jungle fighter from the American forces who had learned everything about stealth and explosives. No one could ever pin you down. No one knew who you were. Many people wanted you dead. Your assassination would have been a tremendous coup. You let your wife die instead."

"And my daughter, Khazar. You're forgetting. My baby daughter. She was small and innocent, Khazar."

"You let them die. It was to have been you."

"It was to have been the three of us."

Khazar shrugged. "In death I will find glory."

Adam shook his head. "I don't think you believe that, Khazar. I think you're just warped through and through. I think your birth was an accident, and your upbringing made you imagine that you can terrorize and torture and kill, and claim it's all noble."

"Who gives a damn what you think, Tchartoff? Now, drop the gun."

Adam shrugged, dropping the gun on the desk. "It's over for you, Khazar. All over."

"Get out of the way."

Adam arched a brow politely, then moved toward the door. Khazar, dragging Amber with him, inched toward the desk. His hold on her eased as he reached for the gun, picked it up and aimed it at Adam's heart.

He was going to shoot. He was going to shoot Adam straight through the heart. She couldn't bear it. No matter how frightened or horrified she had been, she couldn't allow that to happen. She screamed, shoving her arm hard against his. The gun exploded.

But Adam didn't fall. He was already in motion, wrenching her from Khazar's hold, shoving her behind him and toward the door. "Get out, Amber—"

"Adam, you're alive—"

"Amber, the gun was loaded with blanks. I would never have come near Khazar with a loaded gun when he was holding you."

Khazar began to swear savagely at Adam in Arabic. Then his words came in English once again, and he smiled. "It is just us, then—no guns, no knives. Just our hands." He stretched his fingers before him to emphasize his point. "Yes, it has come to this."

Adam kept his eyes locked tightly on Khazar's. He spoke with sharp command. "Amber, get the hell out of here."

"Adam, I—"

"For the love of God, Amber, go. I can't fight him with you here, don't you understand?"

She understood. She was a distraction.

"When I am done with you, I will find her. There is nowhere for her to run. I will find her, and I will kill her," Khazar vowed.

"Amber, he's a liar and a dead man. Run. Get the hell out. Find Daldrin down by the river. Follow it to the boats. And hurry. This place is going to blow sky-high."

"What?"

"Damn you, hurry! It's going to blow."

"Blow! Adam, I can't leave you—"

"Go!"

Tears stung her eyes. She had to go; she realized that. It was his only chance. She hurried for the door, then paused. "Adam, I love you."

He didn't reply, and suddenly Khazar made an animal grunting sound and flung himself at Adam.

Amber tore out of the room. She raced down the hallway and tried several doors. She couldn't just run away; she had to find a weapon—she had to rescue Adam.

The doors were all locked; the compound seemed to be deserted. She ran at last into the garden, praying that she might find Daldrin or one of the other American prisoners, praying that she did not encounter one of Khazar's men.

The garden was empty.

She started down the trail, screaming. Someone leaped out of the brush, accosting her. She started to scream. "Stop, Miss Larkspur, I'm here to help you. We need to reach the river."

She pulled back, looking at the man. He was young, with sandy hair and hazel eyes, and wearing the worn remnants of a business suit. He was somewhat gaunt, but he was good-looking, like the boy next door.

"We have to go back. We have to get a gun and go back. Are you one of the military men?"

He shook his head and smiled wryly. "No, I'm a banker. What the hell they ever wanted with bankers..." He shrugged. "You have to come with me. *Now*. We've only got a few minutes left."

"What?"

"We have to get out. The place is set to blow. Come on."

"No, no! Adam is still there."

He stared at her unhappily and tapped his watch. "Tchartoff said to leave by eleven. And he said to take you."

"No!" She wrenched herself away from him. "I have to help Adam!"

The words had barely left her mouth when the earth shuddered violently. The young all-American in the business suit leaped forward, covering her shoulders, bringing her down to the ground. Just as he did, dirt and foliage flew as the compound behind them exploded, sending fire and rock and concrete into the sky.

It was all coming apart. The earth shivered anew.

"We've got to get to the river!" the young man yelled frantically. He stood, pulling Amber to her feet. An explosion rent the air again. Amber screamed, looking on the chaos that had once been a building. Adam. Adam was in there. Adam might well be just so much charred wreckage, like the pieces of building raining from the sky.

"Miss Larkspur, we've got to go!"

She was numb. She couldn't move. He gave her a sudden shove, and she slipped off her feet, landing hard on her buttocks and sliding fast down the incline just as she had before. She splashed into the river, and the cold water brought her to her senses. Adam had come for her. He had managed to take care of Khazar's men and release the prisoners. The compound had seemed empty except for him and Khazar, and then it had exploded....

The young man landed beside her with a heavy splash. He caught her arm. "Come on!"

It wasn't an invitation that left her any choice. She staggered up, and they walked together through the shallow water to the falls, where they walked through the first set of rapids, then slipped on the slimy footing. The water carried them over smooth stones, and then over a second incline. The sound of the water rang more fiercely, and it rushed around Amber, slapping into her mouth until she choked. She was tossed and turned, but she really didn't care; she couldn't feel anything.

And then suddenly she found herself in a quiet, sandy pool, and though the water continued to flow, its force was gone. She breathed in deeply, tasting salt strongly on her lips. She looked out and realized that they had come to the sea. As she staggered up, she saw a small cruiser moving toward them from the open water.

She stared at it, not moving.

The young man rose behind her and touched her arms. "It's one of ours, Miss Larkspur. Can you swim?"

Still numb, she nodded. He took her arm, leading her. She staggered with him until the water deepened. Mechanically, she began to swim.

Twenty minutes later, strong arms pulled her from the water. She looked up into an old and trusted face, Ian Daldrin's face. She stared at him searchingly, then burst into tears. He wrapped his arms around her, along with a warm blanket.

"She's in shock," someone whispered.

"No, no," she protested. "Adam. Adam is back there."

"It's all right," Daldrin told her. "You're safe, Amber. They're radioing your father. He'll meet us in St. Thomas. You'll be all right."

"Did Adam make it out?" she asked desperately.

"He might have. There are other boats, Amber. Someone might pick him up."

She shook her head. Daldrin was patronizing her. "It exploded. The whole place exploded." Her voice dropped to a whisper. "And he was in it!"

"He might have made it out." Daldrin looked around. "Someone get some water. Please. Quickly." He smiled awkwardly at her. She realized that he was soaking wet, too, that he had swum out to be rescued, too. She wanted to smile, because she was so proud of him; he had never faltered. He and Adam were two of a kind. Adam might have grown into his golden years just like Daldrin, dignified . . . noble. He might have. They'd had a chance . . . a fleeting chance.

Daldrin was wonderful; the businessman was wonderful; the crew was wonderful. Even the Navy doctor who shot her full of sedatives was wonderful, but no sedative in the world could lighten her heart.

The sedative did knock her out for the twenty-four hours it took the cruiser to bring them to St. Thomas. There she found herself in a luxury hotel. She managed to wash her hair and wrap herself in a warm terry robe while she awaited her father.

When he arrived, she threw herself into his arms, and he held her as if she was the most precious creation in the entire world. She tried to smile for him, but she only burst into tears. He didn't speak; he just held her, rocking her.

That night the daring rescue of the prisoners from the terrorists was big news. The reporters were kept away from her, but the news of the break was out.

And Peter arrived in St. Thomas, desperate to see her.

"I—I don't want to see him," she said at first. She didn't want to see anyone but Adam. She didn't even want to be distracted from worrying about him.

"Amber, he's an old friend, if nothing else, and he's come a long way. He was sick with worry. He was calling every five minutes when we learned that you had been taken, too. See him."

And so Amber saw him. Her father had bought her plenty of clothes, so she met Peter wearing an island print halter dress, with her hair soft and straight and clean, and her professionally tended and bandaged feet up on a coffee table. When he entered the room, he was so tall, so good-looking, with his awkward, little-boy smile, and so concerned, that she wondered why her heart didn't react more strongly. She hugged him and held him close, thanking him for caring. But it felt alien to be in his arms. And when he started saying feverishly that they could be married right away, that he would never let her out of his sight again, she pulled away and stared at him with a sad smile. "No, Peter. No."

"What? Oh, Amber, I know I was wrong. I should have come around before this. I've been thinking only of myself. And you're upset, so upset—"

"Peter, no. I can't marry you."

"We'll talk later."

"No. I won't marry you, Peter. Ever. I'm sorry. I love you as a dear, dear friend, but I'm not in love with you anymore."

"I can change—" he started to promise.

It hurt. It hurt to see his loss, his confusion, his pain, but she couldn't take them away. "Peter, thank you. Thank you for coming to me, for being glad that I'm alive. But it's over."

"Amber—"

"No, Peter. But hold me for a minute. Hold me, because it's so good to have friends."

She thought he was going to protest, that he would go into a rage because she was turning down his proposal and asking for something different. He opened his mouth as if to speak, and then he held her as she had requested.

Maybe we've both grown up over this, she thought. His cheeks, she noticed later, were damp. So were her own.

She stayed in St. Thomas with her father for three days, resting, letting her feet mend. She found out that the young banker who had helped her in the jungle had a wife and three children, and she arranged for a giant smoked Virginia ham with all the trimmings to be sent to his family as a thank you. She received a phone call from his wife that night, thanking her. "He told me that the men were all very proud of you, that Daldrin told them how you were taken because you were fighting for him.''

"I was screaming," Amber corrected dryly.

"Well, anyway, I'm very proud of you, too, and Jimmy, of course, and all the others. And I've warned him that he's out of international banking! He can handle money right here at home from here on out!''

They talked for a few more minutes, then Amber hung up.

She and her father took an air force flight to Washington. They had barely boarded when her father began to clear his throat. "Amber, I saw—I saw Tchartoff last night."

"What?"

"I saw Adam. He's alive. He even managed to get Khazar out." He hesitated. "I imagine it was difficult for him—he must have wanted to skewer the bastard. Except that we wanted him badly. We want him to go through the courts. We want him charged with murder and kidnapping and everything else, and we're hoping to get more of an insight into the operation. It must have taken a lot of courage and willpower to keep the man alive with everything exploding around them both. But he did it. He dragged Khazar out. They were picked up on the shore the day before yesterday."

"Why—" She had to moisten her lips, had to try very hard to breathe normally. "Why didn't you tell me that he was alive right away? Why—why didn't he come to see me?"

"He—he didn't want to get involved with the press. He said he had to have some time alone, and he asked me to understand. Amber, he did everything we asked him to do. We had to respect his wishes."

"He—he didn't even mention me?" she whispered.

"Yes, he did. He said—" Ted hesitated, staring at the pain in his daughter's eyes. "He said to tell you that he loved you. And that you should have a good and wonderful life."

"That's all?"

Ted nodded miserably.

Amber leaned her head against the window of the plane. For long moments she stared without seeing. Then silent tears started to trickle down her cheeks. She ignored them until her father awkwardly offered her a tissue. He put his arm around her, and she cried on his shoulder until her tears finally dried.

"Honey, it will pass," he promised her.

"No," she said softly. "No. No, it never will."

New York City, New York
July 3

He had been sitting in the living room for hours, Toni thought as she entered her apartment. She'd been shopping. She'd managed to find some great steaks down at the corner market, and she wanted to make a really wonderful dinner for him, to see him smile for just a few minutes.

She wasn't sure why he had come to see her. Most of the time, when he was like this, he just disappeared. He set out by himself on the water, or he found a mountain somewhere in the world and clambered to the top of it.

This time was different. He read the papers voraciously.

Maybe that was it.

A touch of excitement seized hold of Toni. Maybe it was the woman. She'd read all the accounts of the rescue. Adam had never given an interview, but his name was in every story. He was a hero, but he didn't like being called one. He had told her bluntly that he'd done what was necessary, and that was that.

He, too, had read all the accounts, every single thing that appeared. And he didn't like to read about himself, so it had to be . . . the woman.

She must really be something, that daughter of Ted Larkspur. First trying to rescue the senator, then surviving on that island, nearly escaping on her own and all . . . She must have a great deal of fire. Toni smiled. Yes, she must have something.

"Adam, I'm home."

"Good," he said. He didn't mean it. He couldn't care less whether she was around or not.

"How about a Scotch?"

"Fine, thanks."

"I've got some wonderful steaks."

"I'll take you out for dinner."

"No, thanks. I like my dates to notice I'm around."

He rose and came striding into the kitchen. His sandy hair was clean and brushed back. He wore a denim shirt and jeans, and his hands were stuffed idly into his back pockets. "Toni, if I've been a bore, I'm sorry—"

"You're sorry? Adam, why start now?" She laughed. She poured him a nice large Scotch and handed it to him with a wicked grin. "Adam, I think you should get out of here tomorrow."

"What?"

"I know there's a shuttle flight to Washington at 9:00 a.m. It's a holiday, so it will be a real bitch to get you on it, but I have a few friends at the airlines."

"Toni, what are you—"

She plunked down her glass and leaned over the counter. "Adam, think about it. You've always needed a damn heroine. And they don't grow on trees. She's there. I think she means a lot to you, and I think you ought to go and tell her."

His jaw locked, his teeth grated, and for a second Toni thought that he was going to hit her. Except that he would never strike her, not in anger. Not ever. He exhaled. Then the tension faded from his face, and he grinned, shyly, awkwardly.

"Toni, I can't just walk back into her life. I have to give her time."

"You don't have to give her anything."

"She had a fiancé—"

"So the papers say. But they split up before she ever got on the *Alexandria*, and I can read between the lines, even if you can't. Go to her, Adam. Tell her how you feel. Let her know, give her a chance. Give *yourself* a chance."

He stared at her for a moment, then turned without replying.

"Adam!" she called after him. "Adam, what are you doing now?" she asked in dismay.

He paused and looked at her. "Packing, Toni. You say there's a plane at nine?"

A broad smile slowly curved her lips. "Yes, at nine."

"Want to make a reservation?"

"Yes, yes, I do!" He smiled, and she picked up the phone to call the airline. He started toward her tiny guest room to pack his belongings.

Washington, D.C.
July 4

The capitol was gearing up for the independence celebration. From her father's town house window, Amber could see floats going by, tying up traffic, bringing the busy city disastrously near to a halt. She smiled, wondering what the founding fathers would think if they were here now.

There were activities all day long at the White House, and naturally Ted Larkspur was involved. He had wanted Amber to be with him. He had tried to bribe her as if she was still a child, telling her about the fireworks that were planned. She had begged off, and she thought he'd understood. She didn't seem to have the energy to do much. She liked the town house; she liked being alone.

It was still incredible to realize that she was free. And it was incredible to realize that she had been away from Adam for days. She still felt as if a limb had been cut away.

The phone started to ring. She let it. So many of her friends were calling her, concerned, eager to hear her voice. She would call them all back, but not yet. She had given the press a story. She was done with them, for the moment. She needed this time for herself.

The machine answered the phone. She heard her father's voice, asking the caller to leave a message. Then she paused, hearing a voice she didn't recognize at all. It was a woman's voice, soft, pretty, breathless.

"Amber...Miss Larkspur, you don't know me, and I'm going to try to talk very fast and make sense at the same time. My name is Toni, and I'm Adam's cousin. Maybe I shouldn't be calling you, but he's on his way to see you, and this is none of my business, but he might be feeling awkward—"

By then Amber had the receiver in her hand. "Toni! This is Amber Larkspur. You said that Adam... How is he?"

"He's fine. He— Oh, he'd probably have me boiled in ancient oil if he knew that I was on the phone with you, and it was almost impossible to get this number! I'm rambling—I'm sorry. I just— Oh, gosh, this is really going badly, isn't it?"

"No, no, whatever you have to say, thank you for calling me," Amber said quickly.

"He's on his way," Toni said in a rush.

"Here?"

"Yes. I wanted you to know because—because he wants you to be happy, I think. And because I think you should know that—that he really loves you. Before he says anything to you. I just—I just wanted you to know. It's awfully hard for him. He's hurt so badly for so long. I don't know what I'm trying to say to you. Yes, I do. Every hero needs a heroine, that's all. He took the nine o'clock out. Heavens, it's already eleven. It took me longer to drive back from the airport and come up with the courage to call you than it will take him to arrive.''

"He left at nine and it's eleven now?" Amber said.

"Toni, I have to go." She started to hang up. She drew the receiver to her ear. "Thank you, Toni, thank you."

She slammed down the phone. She was in a terry robe, her hair wrapped in a towel. Adam was coming. What should she wear? Her hair, her hair first . . .

He loved her. His cousin had said that he loved her, and that he was coming to her.

She started for her bedroom. She paused with a gasp as the doorbell rang. Him? Already? She raced for the door and stared through the peephole.

It was Adam. Tall, handsome, in a black and white knit shirt and form-hugging jeans. He shifted awkwardly from one foot to the other. He looked at the bell again, then pressed it.

She didn't dare take the time to get dressed. He might disappear again, and she wouldn't be able to stand that. She would go stark raving mad and spend the rest of her life screaming.

She threw open the door, the towel on her head beginning to lean precariously. "Adam!"

He smiled, slowly, awkwardly. It didn't matter what she had on; she knew that. "Amber. Can I come in?"

She threw the door wide. He stepped into the entryway, and looked around. It was a nice place, an old home where politicians had been living for over a century. The entryway was marble, and beyond it the carpeting was soft and inviting. The furniture was Colonial and subdued. It was a nice place, warm and quiet, like her father. She loved the place, and as she noticed his light-blue eyes moving quickly around in appraisal, she knew that he liked it, too.

Then his eyes were on her, and for a long moment they stared at one another. Then, to her horror, Amber felt hot, wet tears rising into her eyes, then gushing from them. "Why?" she whispered. "Why did you leave me?"

She didn't know if she stepped toward him or he stepped toward her, or maybe it didn't matter. She was in his arms, and the unbalanced towel had fallen from her hair. She was muttering things against his chest, sobbing so hard that he couldn't possibly understand.

He kissed her lips, kissed the tears away, then swept her into his arms and carried her to the parlor, where he sat on the sofa, cradling her against his chest.

"Amber, I...I don't know. Maybe I had a few things to figure out myself. Maybe I wanted to give you a chance to forget me, in case it wasn't real, in case it was just circumstances. Maybe...maybe I was afraid. I don't know. But I..." His voice trailed away.

Amber pushed against his shoulder, sitting up straighter and staring into his eyes. The frost was completely gone from them. She had never seen them more open, more vulnerable. He touched her cheek gently. "I was thinking about a house in the Blue Ridge. Something on a mountain, or maybe in a valley. A small valley. I want a place with land, lots of land. With horses and dogs and some good mouse-catching cats. I was thinking about—about children. A tribe maybe, six or seven. Well, I'd be satisfied with one or two, I guess. That's all negotiable. I—'' He paused, meeting her eyes for the longest time, and then he smiled. He picked up her hand, turned it over and tenderly kissed the palm.

Then he met her eyes again. "Amber, you gave me more than life. You gave me peace. And, most important of all, you gave me the gift I had never thought could be mine again. Love. Amber, will you marry me?"

Outside, the first of many explosions took place.

Maybe it hadn't been outside. Maybe it had happened right there, inside her heart.

She leaned forward and kissed him. "Yes."

His heart quickened beneath her hand. "I'm probably not easy to live with," he warned her. "I've given it a lot of thought, and I plan to change my citizenship again. It shouldn't be difficult. Your father owes me. I'll never turn my back on Israel, but the United States gave me a real home when no other country would. What else? I swear like a truck driver in Russian, but maybe that won't be so bad."

"Unless the children learn to speak Russian," Amber corrected. "Then you'll have to tone it down."

"Yes."

She leaned over and kissed him again. Fireworks were exploding across the city. It was the Fourth of July.

Ali Abdul had meant to start his executions that day. Instead, he had passed on to the afterlife himself, and Khazar was in a high-security prison. The captives were all safe, and today was truly a celebration of freedom.

His lips broke away from hers. "Amber, truly, I love you," he whispered. She smiled, loving the intensity in his eyes, the timbre of his voice, the slight quiver in it.

The future might well be stormy, she knew. But she knew, too, that he would always love her with passion, with loyalty, with all his heart and his being. To be loved so deeply was worth any tempest in the world.

"The fireworks are starting already," she whispered.

He nodded, his eyes never leaving hers. "Would you like to go see them?"

She shook her head. "No. I . . . well . . . I much prefer the variety that you—that you create."

He rose, lifting her high in his arms. "Which way?"

She smiled, directing him to her room. He paused in the hallway. "Amber, your father . . . ?"

"He won't be back until late. And if he did come home, Adam, I really don't think he would mind."

Adam smiled. Maybe Larkspur wouldn't mind after all. It had seemed all right that night he had seen him in St. Thomas. He was just happy to have Amber alive. The man had been almost humble.

Then she reached her arms around his neck, pulled his head down to her and kissed his lips, her tongue slipping between his teeth and sensually sliding into his mouth. His breath was quickening, his heart was thundering. . . .

Alive. Yes, she made him feel very much alive.

The door was ahead of them. Her robe was falling open, and the fullness of her breast was there before his eyes. He had to touch her, had to make love with her, had to find life in the never-ending warmth of her arms.

He nudged open the bedroom door with his foot, closed it with his back and held her close with one hand while he slid the bolt with the other.

"Just in case," he whispered.

"We'll make sure he knows your intentions are honorable," Amber drawled lazily.

"You're an awful minx," he told her, but when he laid her down on the bed and spread open her robe, his breath caught, and then he stretched out beside her and held her close. "No," he murmured. "A heroine. A beautiful, beautiful heroine."

She opened her arms to him with a smile that was both wistful and provocative. "Heroines need their heroes," she whispered. Her voice was a caress. It touched his flesh with warmth, with passion. It seared his heart and his loins, and he wondered how he had ever managed to stay away from her for so long.

He kissed her. He listened to the fireworks exploding all around them, and his lips fell to her breast. She was sweet and beautiful, and the clean, perfumed scent of her flesh aroused him even further.

But he made love to her slowly. He savored every taste and scent and touch. He felt her lips upon him, and the caress of her hands, felt the bounty of her body beneath him.

She met his eyes. "Fireworks!" she whispered.

He curled her tight into his arms. "And every day the Fourth of July," he returned.

She smiled and rolled above him, her hair falling across his chest. "*Shalom*, my love," she whispered. "Welcome. Welcome home."

Epilogue

It was a quiet wedding. At least, it had been intended to be quiet.

But as with many such things, the guest list had gotten a bit out of hand, and there were reporters, and the curious, and somehow all of them managed to attend. The bride was dressed in a beautiful white gown with a long, flowing train and incredible work done in beads and sequins. She was tall and majestic and blond, and she had the appearance of a true princess.

The groom was striking in his tux. Tall, straight, handsome and, really, all the wonderful things that the prince who wed such a princess should be.

The church was decked out with a multitude of flowers, and there was beautiful music. It was rumored that even the president was in attendance, and, of course, that meant security and even more confusion.

The bride's father's eyes seemed a little damp as he handed her over to the groom. And yet, when his eyes met the groom's, he seemed confident that he couldn't have found a better man to whom to give his daughter.

Actually, Ted Larkspur thought, listening to the vows being exchanged between his daughter and Adam Tchartoff, he *had* found Adam Tchartoff. He'd gone to great lengths to find the man.

And now . . . this.

The justice of the peace told Adam that he could kiss his bride. To cheers, Adam did so. Ted exhaled. It was done. His daughter was married.

The newlyweds turned and walked down the aisle.

The reception was held at Ted's home in Alexandria. The catering bill had been exorbitant, but he had only one daughter, and he had wanted her to cherish this day forever. Of course, she would have done so even if she had been married in the house with no witnesses but himself and Toni. Still, this had been important to him.

They danced in the garden under the stars. He held her close to him, and he felt his eyes fill with tears again. He wasn't losing a daughter, he was gaining a son, he reminded himself. If anyone deserved Amber for a lifetime, it was Tchartoff. He had saved her life.

And still . . .

"There's a rumor going around that the groom is going to take a post in Washington," he whispered to Amber.

She arched a brow and smiled. He'd never seen a more beautiful bride. Ever. Even if she was his daughter.

"Yes, he's going to take the job, Dad." She sighed. "It would be a waste to keep him away. He's so knowledgeable, and with all his languages..." She shrugged. "But the house is only an hour's commute. I want him home nights."

Ted smiled. "Amber, if you think I'm going to have any control over your husband..."

She laughed. "Okay, then, I'll warn you. I'm going to make sure he has no wish to work nights."

"Ouch. Careful, my ears are tender!" Ted moaned. "I can still remember when you were in diapers, you know."

"Diapers. Yes, that's the idea."

"What?"

"Don't you want to be a grandfather?" Those sea-green eyes were on him, beautiful, mischievous.

He would have answered her, except the groom cut in just then. "Excuse me, sir!"

The two of them waltzed away. It was just as it should be; Ted knew that.

The president came up and slapped Ted on the back. "Congratulations. It seemed we were in the midst of disaster, and now it's turned to triumph."

Ted nodded. "Yes." He was silent for a moment. "Grandchildren! They're talking about grandchildren."

The president laughed. "Mm. Just think, they will be part Russian. Your grandchildren will be part Russian."

"And Austrian. And American—"

"Yes, all-American," the president agreed, laughing.

Ted glanced at him, then smiled slowly and looked across the lawn, where the two were still dancing, beautiful, graceful, raptured by one another. "Grandchildren. Actually I think I rather like the idea. Yes, I like it very much. She could have a little girl, just like herself. A beautiful little girl."

Washington, D.C.
May 24

The call reached Ted Larkspur at 4:00 a.m.

"It's a boy, sir. Michael Theodore Tchartoff. He was nine pounds, one ounce, and he has a head full of blond hair. Blue eyes, at the moment. Oh, and he can kick like a linebacker."

Ted allowed the phone to drop for a moment, a smile as broad as the Atlantic stretching across his features.

A boy...

He couldn't wait to see his grandson. They could play ball in the park.

No, the grandchildren idea wasn't bad at all.

"Adam, congratulations!" he said quickly. "And Amber?"

"Amber is just fine. We're still in the delivery room. She's right next to me. Want to talk to her?"

"No," Ted said. He laughed. "Tell her I'm on my way!"

A boy. Michael Theodore Tchartoff.

He liked it! It was an all-American name if he'd ever heard one, and it was just right for his grandson.

*   *   *   *   *

A celebration of motherhood by three of your favorite authors!

Birds, Bees and Babies

JENNIFER GREENE
KAREN KEAST
EMILIE RICHARDS

This May, expect something wonderful from Silhouette Books — BIRDS, BEES AND BABIES — a collection of three heartwarming stories bundled into one very special book.

It's a lullaby of love . . . dedicated to the romance of motherhood.

Look for BIRDS, BEES AND BABIES in May at your favorite retail outlet.

®

You'll flip . . . your pages won't!
Read paperbacks *hands-free* with

Book Mate • I

The perfect "mate" for all your romance paperbacks
Traveling • Vacationing • At Work • In Bed • Studying
• Cooking • Eating

Perfect size for all standard paperbacks, this wonderful invention makes reading a pure pleasure! Ingenious design holds paperback books OPEN and FLAT so even wind can't ruffle pages—leaves your hands free to do other things. Reinforced, wipe-clean vinyl-covered holder flexes to let you turn pages without undoing the strap . . . supports paperbacks so well, they have the strength of hardcovers!

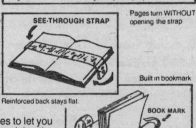

Pages turn WITHOUT opening the strap

SEE-THROUGH STRAP

Reinforced back stays flat.

Built in bookmark

BOOK MARK

BACK COVER HOLDING STRIP

10˝ x 7¼˝, opened.
Snaps closed for easy carrying, too

Available now. Send your name, address, and zip code, along with a check or money order for just $5.95 + .75¢ for postage & handling (for a total of $6.70) payable to Reader Service to:

Reader Service
Bookmate Offer
901 Fuhrmann Blvd.
P.O. Box 1396
Buffalo, N.Y. 14269-1396

Offer not available in Canada
*New York and Iowa residents add appropriate sales tax.

BM-G

AVAILABLE NOW—

the books you've been waiting for by one of
America's top romance authors!

DIANA PALMER

DUETS

Ten years ago Diana Palmer published her very first
romances. Powerful and dramatic, these gripping tales
of love are everything you have come to expect from
Diana Palmer.

This month some of these titles are available again in
DIANA PALMER DUETS—a special three-book collection. Each book has two wonderful stories plus an intro-
duction by the author. You won't want to miss them!

Book 1
SWEET ENEMY
LOVE ON TRIAL

Book 2
STORM OVER THE LAKE
TO LOVE AND CHERISH

Book 3
IF WINTER COMES
NOW AND FOREVER

Available now at your favorite retail outlet.

Silhouette Books®

DP-1A